THE DARKNESS CALL

Gary Fincke

THE DARKNESS CALL

PLEIADES
P R E S S

Robert C. Jones Short Prose Series

Warrensburg, Missouri

Library of Congress Control Number:
ISBN 978-0-8071-8690-5

Published by Pleiades Press

Department of English
University of Central Missouri
Warrensburg, Missouri 64093

Distributed by Louisiana State University Press

Cover Image: "Casablanca" (classic version). Aldwyth. Collage on
Okawara paper, 78.5 x 71". 2003-6
Photographer of the cover image: Rick Rhodes
Book design by Sarah Nguyen
Author's photo by Jonathan MacBride
First Pleiades Printing, 2018

Financial support for this project has been provided by the University
of Central Missouri and the Missouri Arts Council, a state agency.

Table of Contents

THE PHYSICS OF DESIRE

The spacecraft Planck is the coldest known object in space, including dust and gas.

Pictures

My father, hands on his walker, stays seated in his chair with the fabric-covered arms so sweat-soiled the pattern has been erased. The small, decades-old television shows darkness. He says, "You try" as if I might resurrect the guests he says he watches until he sleeps. This morning, the second week of weather too warm even for July, his lawn is infested with a widespread eczema of flowering weeds. Every window in his house with no air conditioning is closed and locked.

Voyager

As always, I am working at faith. Stars, I've just read, must be three billion years old in order for complex life to evolve on one of their planets, and even then, need the luck of the Goldilocks Effect, the neither too hot nor too cold porridge of atmosphere stirred with water and age.

Years beyond gravity, Voyager II, launched in 1977, carries a golden record with sounds and images that are meant to represent us to residents of distant planets. It speeds that news toward aliens we have imagined since Ezekiel, the four-faced, four-winged creatures he witnessed setting early standards for extraterrestrial invaders.

The Time Throat

Along the Susquehanna River, last week, a man I'd once worked with chattered me through thistle and milkweed to where the water widened and turned shallow enough to surface what looked to be a bridge of stones. A month earlier, the water running higher, an evangelist concentrating on where his feet were placed could have seemed a temporary Christ, but my former colleague meant me to believe in a red carpet for aliens who are speeding to us via a time tunnel, one that will open next to the stones he and other believers had laid.

Ufology 1

A hundred years ago, photographs of cardboard cutouts of fairies copied from a children's book were taken by two young girls, Elise Wright and Frances Griffiths. They were circulated through the celebrity of Arthur Conan Doyle as proof of the reality of fairies. A century later, the heavens are clouded by visitors from other galaxies. Abductions, now, are so common only the friends and relatives of the snatched are excited. In each story, the kidnapped undergo a physical exam. In every saga, their possessions are taken—a watch, a cell phone, a wallet. The items are hoarded by the aliens as if they were relics to be worshipped like a shroud, holy splinters, or the bits and pieces of saints and martyrs.

Planck in Space

The space ship Planck has been traveling for years on a mission to measure what remains of the Big Bang's transformational light. By now it is the coldest object in space, near absolute zero, its name making me look up Max Planck, the physicist, his theorem I memorized in high school. I find a comment attributed to Planck's teacher in 1880: "Physics is finished, young man. It's a dead end street." Now, when I try to decipher Planck's Constant, the way to measure the tiniest spark of energy, calculated to 10^{-34} given off by the minutest bits of matter, I feel helpless.

Relics

Our Italian tour guide, last summer, cited the wealth of the Catholic church, how it has supported the reassuring propaganda of religious art. For centuries here, she said, just the one choice, and led us into our third cathedral of the day, where, she said, we would see parts of St. Catherine, a virgin, dead, like Christ, at thirty-three, but blessed, during her lifetime, with the stigmata.

Ufology 2

In October 1955, in Kentucky, when the unearthly light wavered across the McGehee's harvested field, the little green invaders were armed. They laid a perimeter around the farmhouse, and unprovoked, fired their alien bullets, but luckily the McGehees owned four shotguns and didn't hesitate to use them, saving themselves and presumably, us, the green midgets retreating to blast off for a planet where household defense has been outlawed, some peace-loving place easily conquered, its inhabitants nothing like the honest, sober, and religious McGehees, who swore on their personal, family Bibles every fantastic word was true.

The Time Throat

The universe, my former colleague said, is scattered through with throats, and one of those mouths, miraculously, empties here. For work, years ago, he taught two languages; for faith, he spoke as if he were certain that I was worthy of secrets. "Like a worm hole?" I said, looking at the sky above the Susquehanna as if a funnel cloud of calm might descend.

Ufology 3

In Roswell, New Mexico, in the UFO museum, there are models of thin-faced, enormous-eyed aliens like the ones who supposedly crashed there in 1947. In photos, a host of shadows and glare alongside the testimonies of sober pilots and recent Presidents—Jimmy Carter claiming the space ship was big and bright and moon-sized, Ronald Reagan's plane buzzed by a speeding white light. In the busy UFO gift shop, an alien ceramic teenager; an alien head lamp; alien bobble heads, large and small; all of them with the same emaciated, black-eyed face.

Voyager

Carl Sagan added his lover's pulse and breath to Voyager's golden record, recording the brainwaves of Ann Druyan, who concentrated on what it's like to fall in love: Kisses and laughter. Footsteps. Heartbeats. She trusted the aliens to understand human passion after they cracked the mysterious code for the physiology of desire.

Pictures

As if, after death, her body could be photo shopped, my father, for twenty-five years, has prepared to reunite with the version of my mother he touched before my birth, believing that he, in turn, will be seen by her as young and fit.

Relics

St. Catherine wrote of experiencing a "mystical marriage with Jesus." She claimed to receive Communion directly from Christ and chose to abstain from eating because fasting led to holiness. Her frequent, prolonged refusals of food likely led to her death.

Planck in Space

Millions of miles from here, the spaceship Planck is equipped to show the origin of ourselves with instruments so perfect they could, from Earth, detect the heat of a rabbit upon the moon.

Ufology 4

"Life exists on other planets and we will find it within twenty years," the scientist Andrei Finkelstein said last year. He explained that ten percent of known planets circling suns in the galaxy resemble Earth, so many chances for life on such planets that it was impossible not to believe the aliens thrived. Furthermore, he said, the aliens are most likely to resemble humans with two arms, two legs, and a head. Finkelstein made the remarks at the opening of the international symposium called "The Search for Extraterrestrial Intelligence" in St. Petersburg.

Voyager

By the time Voyager left the solar system, Sagan was years dead. Druyan, unhooking her lace-trimmed bra or sliding off a slip, might have recollected how Sagan imagined the lingerie of another planet, how the era of intimate contact would begin when her recorded desire, at last, approached the distant, intelligent discoverers.

The Time Throat

"Worm hole is such an uninformative name," my former colleague said, so dismissive that I kept to myself what I'd recently read, that there was a theory, now, that employed worm holes of "Planck length," a distance of about 10^{-20} the diameter of a proton. Thus, the writer had said, "extremely small."

Planck in Space

If everything goes as planned, the instruments on board the spaceship Planck will draw up a map of the Cosmos as it appeared thirteen billion years ago, as close to the moment of "first light" as is possible. That first light is also known as "relic radiation."

Pictures

My father shows me a photograph labeled "McConnell's Mills, 1939," my mother in a bathing suit, thin and pretty, smiling. He turns to "1940, North Park," my mother holding a tennis racket, a sagging net behind her. In another, dressed in the same short-skirted tennis outfit, she is seated at a picnic table holding a slice of watermelon with both hands.

Relics

In the Basilica of San Domenico, the guide said St. Catherine was so important there was a rivalry between cities for her remains. Her body, she said, is elsewhere now, but the head and thumb are here before you, her face still well-preserved through the compassionate grace of God. We shuffled past the sarcophagus roped off from the eager who might be tempted to touch. St. Catherine's thumb was displayed close by. Her head was shown so far away I had to squint to see it clearly.

Ufology 5

Stephen Hawking has warned humans to beware of alien contact in a recent Discovery Channel series titled, "Into the Universe with Stephen Hawking." The episode with his caution imagines a scenario of alien life forms coming to Earth in enormous spaceships, on the hunt for resources after draining their planet dry. Hawking says that "If aliens visit us, the outcome would be the same as when Columbus landed in America, which didn't turn out well for the Native Americans." He says that humans should cease efforts to contact alien life, such as the 2008 NASA experiment that sent the Beatles song "Across the Universe" into space.

Pictures

In its own box, what looks to be the original from the studio, a framed photograph of my mother in her wedding dress, November 27, 1941. The war is ten days away. My father says, "I want you to know where I keep these."

Planck in Space

The spaceship Planck will detect what remains of that original light when only temperature existed, tracking theory to the bright beginning of everything. I imagine the rabbit on the moon, the probe that could dive bomb it like some inter-terrestrial falcon a merciless exhibit for the Natural History of First Things, the solid sky plunged into light that lasts, we're told, forever, so close, now, to God or absence, we watch the chilled instruments for the precise moment of miracle.

Relics

In Siena, while we filed by the boxed thumb of St. Catherine, we watched one of our tour companions, the woman who photographed each meal she ate, slip Euros through a slot to light a candle, and we averted our eyes as she knelt to pray after dipping her fingers into an ornate basin and moving her dripping hand through the sign of the cross.

The Time Throat

"My daughters are grown now," my former colleague said. "They are believers. Like me, they expect to be the first humans seen." When I stayed quiet, he said, "Haven't you always wished to know every secret?" So rapt with anticipation, I listened as if he'd had those daughters hide nearby to begin the song of Sirens, the summer air above the river shimmering for cosmic sailors lured by their ravenous need for worship.

Pictures

"It's the faces on that thing that keep me company," my father says, holding the photograph album, but looking at the blank television screen while I twist dials and push buttons as if I might bring it back to life. "I just need to see them. I don't need the sound to come back."

Voyager

Now that science has stripped nearly everything bare of awe and threatens to make us soulless, our mind's electricity must be deciphered when that disc is played, proving that others dream beyond themselves, that somebody else longs to be entered for love or pleasure. Voyager II, in late 2012, is nearly 10 billion miles from the sun. It will be 40,000 years before it approaches another planetary system. An eternity from us, someone will go home, centuries from now, and undress to embrace, joyous with learning those life-forms that rely upon only two legs share the ecstasy of love.

CATCHING

Miss Klein Explains *Contagious*

Twice a week, during third grade public health, Miss Klein filled the room with fear while we sat in perfect rows marked by small spots in the wax, the ones that revealed restlessness, that shamed if they showed like lace-edged slip hems. The contagious, she said, leave filth that hides on buses and streetcars and seats at the movies. Believe me, you'll never know who's been there and given you the itch and fester.

The contagious never cover their mouths when they sneeze. They wipe their noses on their sleeves where crusts collect like scabs that bleed. The contagious borrow combs and touch fountains with their mouths. They gobble food they've dropped to floors. Not setting rings of paper, they squat on public toilets, never scrub with water that's been run to scalding hot. What's worse, she said, the contagious shout words you mustn't say. They ruin their yards with bottles, cans, and tires. The contagious are everywhere, common as flies. Splattering stains, the contagious spread like lies. Look around. You'll see what I mean. Eyes open, class. Keep yourselves clean. Everything that makes children sick is catching.

Children's Television

In Portugal, once, the script of a children's soap opera called for symptoms of a mysterious disease. Soon there were hundreds of children sick with those symptoms. Episode by episode, the epidemic deepened. Each symptom was completed like homework. Mothers feared their daughters would be permanently pock marked; they followed their sons' geometrical proofs of cough and rash and fever, afraid of its solution. All of them watched until the script declared an end to epidemic. But after every child recovered, after school reopened, someone hinted that a child, next season, would be crushed inside an accident's car.

My Mother Lists the Things that are Catching

Measles. Mumps. Chicken pox.
The flu. The common cold. Strep throat.
Whooping cough. Smallpox. Tuberculosis.
Head lice. Ringworm. Impetigo.
Poison ivy. Poison sumac. Poison oak.
Comic books. Television. Rock and roll.
Lying. Stealing. Cursing. Idle hands.

Tulipomania

In the early seventeenth century, in the Netherlands, tulips, newly arrived from Turkey, charmed everyone. Tulips loved Holland's soil. New breeds were developed. Flowers with vivid colors and dramatic lines and patterns that resembled flames were coveted. The price of bulbs that promised the drama of color went up. Gardens flourished. There were mornings when people awoke to the glory of extraordinary color and needed more tulips.

The best of the hybrid bulbs were named after famous people: Admiral Liefkin, Admiral Van der Eyck, and most expensive and rare, the Semper Augustus, all of them coveted like fantastic, fashionable clothes. The rich had to own the best of those bulbs. It showed bad taste to be without a collection of bulbs. Speculators in tulip bulbs made huge profits. People bought bulbs on credit, eager to be rich.

At last the price of a single bulb rose to as much as the equivalent of two million dollars, until, in 1637, the bubble burst, and the deepest believers were ruined.

The Dangers of Mouth Breathing

Third grade, and yet, so far, I hadn't missed a day of school. I knew what contagious was. I'd had chicken pox and measles at four and five because my older sister had brought those sicknesses home before I'd started school even though she washed her hands in the bathroom and never wiped her nose on her sleeve like I did.

I kept bundled up all winter, wearing boots, a hat with ear flaps, and a scarf my mother choked me with from December through February. But the contagious, my mother reminded me, were sure to get me if I didn't stop breathing through my mouth.

"You look like somebody who will catch everything that's going around," she said.

Or "You look like you're catching flies."

Or "You look retarded."

I was a mouth breather because it felt better. My mouth brought in more air. My nose seemed to be clogged up all the time, and yet nobody in my family said a word about allergies and their consequences. My father had taught me that allergies were for sissies. Dust, pine trees, grass seed, cats—all of those items were so common there had to be something weak in me if I had problems. If I kept my mouth shut, I'd be fine.

I watched movies where somebody was gagged and imagined dying that way, unable to get air through my untouched nose. Other kids held their breath underwater to see who could do it the longest, but I didn't need water to pretend to drown. All I had to do was "lip seal" for a few minutes and I'd feel like I needed to surface.

The doctor said I should put a straw between my lips and keep it there. He didn't say anything about school, when that straw would earn me permanent humiliation. For a few days I kept the straw in place around the house, at least when my parents or my sister might see me. The rest of the time it was in my pocket collecting a film of filth where I'd moistened it with my mouth while I sucked in great gulps of air.

But my mother was right. I had serial sore throats, going off to school scratchy and raw. "Just shut your mouth and keep it shut," my mother said. And I did. For five minutes. For ten. And every time she was close enough to see me.

Chain Letters

Chain letters return like strains of flu, popping up periodically with promises of wealth. One of them, the "send-a-dime," began in Denver, 1935, as the pyramid of replies was expanded by the yeast of greed. Evidence? The postal volume in Denver rose by more than 100,000 items per day. In some cities, "chain-headquarters" opened like flea markets. And within days everyone had a letter to sell, and there was no one left to buy.

The Year before Salk

Miss Klein said polio didn't go away like chicken pox or the measles. You caught it from filth, and you wore braces and used crutches forever. Or worse, you were stuck in an iron lung like the ones she showed us on the screen she tugged down from near the ceiling. There were kids our age who were never going to do anything but lie inside machines that helped them breathe. "Let this be a lesson," Miss Klein said. "Don't ever forget to keep clean."

We brought in a dime every Friday during third grade and slid it into a slot inside a card featuring a smiling child on crutches. Miss Klein kept our cards inside her desk. I loved seeing my card fill up. When there were ten dimes, we started again. "You wash your hands, all of you," Miss Klein said after we slotted our dimes. "God knows who handled those coins. How filthy he was and what you could catch."

When I swam in a lake that summer, my mother ran a hot bath and stuck me in it, telling me to soak for a while. "That's not a swimming pool where germs are killed. I hope you kept that mouth of yours shut in that water," she said. "Just imagine what other kids have done in there. And animals. And everything under the sun."

I still didn't wash my hands or blow my nose every time it began to run, but now I was terrified of lake water. Nearly every one of my friends swam in lakes, yet none of them caught polio that summer. But when fourth grade began, there was Richard Hartman, two years younger, wearing leg braces and using crutches, looking exactly like the children in the ads for the March of Dimes that raised money for polio research. Mrs. Gardiner had new March of Dimes cards for each of us. Jerry Mushik laughed when I washed my hands after I'd inserted my dime. He put his on his tongue and closed his mouth. Richard Hartman didn't seem to be getting any better. The dimes weren't going to help him, my mother said. It's too late for that. Jerry Mushik licked his dime for three straight weeks. In the cloakroom he forced two boys to lick their dimes, and none of them got sick.

Dance Mania

In the thick history of hysteria, Frau Troffea, in 1518, suddenly lifts her arms as if she's hanging sheets on a line to dry in Strasbourg, France. Hallelujah, she could be singing, but then her feet skid into the swerve of dance, limbs chattering out of sync with any tune her neighbors know. There, in the sixteenth century, spectators gather like they do for the first dance at a wedding, but she carries on for days, tranced by some phantom partner who leads until one of those onlookers joins, then another, so many more in this weeks-long fit of dancing, that outdoor ballroom fills four hundred strong, moshers for the inaudible, the song on repeat, the pit keyed to a frenzy of thrashing, each dancer with room enough for solitary violence. Nothing can end this except exhaustion or, for many, death, that manic choreography famous for casualties who endured to the heart's collapse.

Laugh Track

During the years before the laugh track, when the Russians had mastered the atomic bomb, and Pittsburgh, where we lived, was a first-launch target, comedies, in black and white, blinked through the snow on our Dumont's screen. My mother would say "Shhhh" to hush me mute, whatever was funny sealed behind my lips, not to be opened until the commercials came on because I was there to watch and listen, not act the fool.

Some nights the sirens that would signal world's end sounded in tests. Some nights the television paused to remind us to seek shelter when its shows ended for real. But now there were programs, suddenly, where each line was hilarious, laughter rising and falling as often as breath. It sounded like people my mother knew, the chuckles of men in suits, the titters of women who wore dresses and stockings to shop for butter and milk.

My mother began to laugh along. She had company now, but I kept my mouth shut because there was never the laughter of boys, somebody under twelve happy to act the fool. Television was really funny these days, she told me, the sounds returning so often we recognized the laughs as if they came from our neighbors. At home, in living rooms, there were people like us in shorts and t-shirts, underwear and robes, who agreed about humor.

And then, a few of those laughs disappeared as if their owners had sickened or died, replaced in the front row by foreigners. My mother said she could hear the accents of those who spoke Spanish when they wanted her not to hear. Or worse, the snickers of Russians, as if there was laughter coming through those earphones at the U.N. during the daily talk of World War III.

From commercial to commercial, my mother went silent again, listening for strangers, people she said I should fear, who would find us funny when we tried to run, believing the head start we'd had was the only way to save ourselves.

The Laughter Epidemic

In 1962, following a schoolboy's joke, thousands of people in Tanganyika laughed nonstop for months.

Like chicken pox, one joke passed from child to child, the contagious entering their houses to spread the rash of laughter. Villages, within days, housed hilarity. Boys whispered into their fathers' ears, their teeth bared from grinning. Mothers, hugged by daughters, were tickled to cackling. Comedian zero, that jokester, laughed and shook. "A fit," the teacher thought, smiling, as the class snickered at history like generals, each incident a punch line. When school, hysterical, was closed, the children howled as they scattered onto homeward paths, the sound of joy, by now, so widespread, even the surrounding jungle seemed hilarious.

The Devil's Children

"The sins of your fathers," Mrs. Shaffer said, "belong to you," and she listed the ways from drunk to unfaithful while our Sunday school class constructed heaven and hell, silently attaching the future for all of us onto the church's new bulletin boards. Melanie Troxell, whose father was gone, cut narrow spaces into heaven's gate, forming a grate so we could see inside where white wings we drew floated against a cloudless blue sky. We shaped a purple robe for God and a loose, white cloak for Jesus, their faces turned away because we dared not look upon them.

"The whirling of those white wings," Mrs. Shaffer said, "looks like it was created by the sweet, benevolent breath of God."

All of us designed the black wings for hell. Dick Wertz, his father arrested, scissored scarlet triangles for eternal flames and left the green door to hell wide open for the paired hands we made by tracing ours. We forecast weather for hell, heavy rain, every drop vanishing above the

25

flames because not one would ever reach us when God saw into our sinful hearts that year before boys and girls were separated for Sunday School, before we began to learn the secret sins of lust and envy, using the sin of falsehood to deny how we abused ourselves and blasphemed, counting the commandments we broke each day although Mrs. Shaffer made us sit, one by one, beside the dark, detailed face of Satan she drew, learning, each Sunday, how it felt to be the devil's children.

Three Condemnations of Hair

Near the end of the eleventh century, the pope decreed that men with long hair should be excommunicated and no prayers offered for their hell-bound souls after death.

In 1705, in Russia, Peter the Great condemned the beard, levying a tax on the bearded rather than threatening them with hell.

In 1838 the king of Bavaria forbade the mustache, saying those who had one would be arrested and shaved. When all of the mustaches disappeared, no one needed to be arrested.

Self-Contagious

At last, during fourth grade, the worst sore throat I'd ever had kept me home from school. "Now you're like everybody else," my mother said. When it worsened, the doctor made a house call and diagnosed an advanced case of strep throat. He warned that my throat might have been neglected too long. I had a heart murmur and could, if things turned worse, come down with rheumatic fever. My mother, looking terrified, hovered nearby. I knew I could give myself something worse, that I was self-contagious.

Possession

In the 17th century, in Loudun, Mother Superior Jeanne des Agnes claimed the spirit of Urbain Grandier, the parish priest, visited her at night to seduce her. Soon other nuns reported spectral foreplay, moaning in ecstasy at night, convulsing and speaking in tongues during the day. Exorcism followed, but the nuns remained possessed by the demons Asmodeus and Zabulon who had entered the convent with a bouquet of roses thrown over the wall by Grandier. When the trial went public, crowds of thousands came to watch. A third demon that possessed those nuns was named — Isacaron, the devil of debauchery. Out of the nuns' mouths flowed public blasphemy. From the files of the exorcist came the contract from Asmodeus, signed in blood by Grandier, a host of demons, and Satan himself. That contract has been saved for centuries, so that long after Grandier was burned at the stake, those nuns recanting and regaining their holiness, we can witness Satan's pitchforked signature and the decorative names of the demons. That contract, historians are sure, is in the handwriting of Mother Superior Jeanne des Agnes, who claimed sorrow for her lies.

The War of the Worlds

In 1938, on Halloween eve, Orson Welles and the Mercury Theater Company broadcast a play based on H. G. Wells' *The War of the Worlds.* A still-famous panic followed. Martians had landed in New Jersey. People rushed to their cars and packed the roads. They hid in their cellars. They loaded guns. The Martians, who "glistened like wet leather," invaded New York City before Earth's bacteria killed them.

Interviewed after the panic, Orson Welles said he thought the story "so improbable," he was afraid people would be bored. He was surprised that even once in a lifetime a hoax like that could work.

In 1944, *The War of the Worlds* aired again in Santiago, Chile, six years and publicity doing nothing to prevent more heart attacks and injuries from an epidemic of panic.

In 1949, in Quito, someone reread that play, and the duped, when they discovered how they'd been fooled, burned the radio station. In that invasion, twenty people died, the revenge-driven earthlings watching the panicked tumble from upstairs windows, which was what invaders deserved, the fire each time, ask questions later.

The Crusades

One Sunday, just before we were moved to the next "higher" class, Mrs. Shaffer said the Crusades were the pinnacle of holiness. "Imagine," she said, "a host of armies fighting for Christ." She told us about Peter the Hermit, who was the hero who preached so well Christians everywhere joined up to rescue the Holy Land from the heathens.

"There were many crusades," she said, "because the struggle never ends." She explained that for hundreds of years, every Christian wanted to march to Jerusalem, so many volunteers there was always a next Crusade. "And listen," she finally said, "in 1213, there were 30,000 children who marched. Imagine that, boys and girls. Imagine them being willing to be martyrs for Christ."

A Month of Crusaders, 2010

March 29th	Moscow, two women detonate on the Metro, 40 dead
March 31st	Kizlyar, two bombers, 12 dead
March 31st	Khyber, Pakistan, one car bomber, 6 dead
April 4th	Baghdad, three car bombers, 42 dead
April 9th	Ingushetia, Russia, one woman detonates, 2 dead
April 12th	Mosul, Iraq, one car bomber, 3 dead
April 19th	Peshawar, Pakistan, one bomber, 26 dead
April 23rd	Baghdad one car bomber, 11 dead
April 26th	Sana'a, Yemen, one bomber, 1 dead
April 28th	Baghdad, two car bombers, 5 dead

The Martyr in our Town

This week, 2011: July 27th, Iraq, 10 dead. July 30th, Afghanistan, 4 dead.

All of the martyrs seem as far away as famine. In small towns like the one where I live no one expects a martyr who would scout the public places where we gather in great numbers. Who would enter our malls and note the busiest stores; who would scan the food court's longest lines. Who would, on Fridays, watch football at the high school. Who would, on Saturdays, sit through a blockbuster film. Who would, on Sundays, attend church, sitting with families on wooden pews.

In his small apartment he studies prophecies and commandments. He reads only the holy translations. At last, when winter justifies his knee-length coat, he thickens his waist with dynamite, develops a nails and ball-bearings paunch. He enters the one restaurant where every diner has three forks, two spoons, and wine on ice, ticking as he gives his reservation name. He decides that the tables nearby are perfect with use, steps forward as the hostess offers a complimentary hanger for his heavy coat. All this, he prays, will spread, go airborne, a pandemic contagion. She employs the word "sir" just as he triggers himself, ascending.

OPENING THE BONE

The morning of my operation, I read the history of trepanning, how skulls, for eight thousand years, have been drilled to lessen the bone. The world's oldest medical procedure, the books said, but the night before, a student I knew had been bludgeoned with fists and shoes, his skull opened by an older treatment.

At the oral surgeon's, set for surgery that would break bone to put an end to pain, I read a set of sayings from dentists past that were listed on a poster: "A frog tied to the jaw can make teeth firm" was accredited in ancient Rome. "A live mouse held to the gums stops toothache" was prescribed even earlier in Egypt.

Culture by culture, the dentists offered cures, and I looked for the nostrums of the drunk and the brutal, checked for the names of the vicious who have taken the teeth of victims with the simple assault of anger. And there, just before the lowest item on the poster sank into shadow behind the bowed head of a woman who was waiting for her own oral corrections was "Scratch painful gums with the teeth of a man who has died violently," but I could not see who was given credit for that prescription, not even when I rose, for my standing straightened her in her chair as if she thought my hands were the animals of bad advice.

HEARTS

1

In space, the hearts of astronauts become rounder. According to the scientists who have studied this phenomenon, the hearts of those who spend long periods of time in space were transformed into a shape that averaged nearly 10% more spherical after six months.

2

In Minnesota, recently, the hearts of moose have so often faltered too soon, they've suffered a cluster of early mortality so profound that they have been wired and followed from a distance by veterinarians. When interviewed, one of them explained that when a moose heart stops beating, it sends a text message to their phones that says, "I'm dead at x and y coordinates," directing them so quickly to the downed, they have a better chance to decipher the clumsy heart.

3

My sister, who has examined the human heart in the commonplace of gravity, has prepared herself for surgery on her own faulty heart. The doctor is a friend, the anesthetist a colleague. A volunteer for study, she has already been monitored a dozen ways, details of her heart and the outcomes of her surgery to become averages or anomalies.

4

One afternoon, during eighth grade, I stood with my classmates around the cow's heart Miss Hutchings unwrapped on her desk. Inside and out, she said, we need to know ourselves, halving that heart to show us auricles, ventricles, valves, the wall well-built or else. Her fingers found where arteries begin. She pressed the ends of veins. She said we were learning the circulatory system the proper way, observing first hand.

5

That cow's heart Miss Hutchings displayed looked nothing like the ones that had been suggested on Valentine's Day, during cartoons, and in art classes, beginning in first grade with Mrs. McIntyre having us draw a sweeping arc from near the top of our red, folded construction paper down to the very bottom. "Now cut, children," she said, "very carefully along that line and then unfold." And though some of them were V-shaped and others looked more like balls, in a minute all of us had the suggestion of a bright red heart to write, "I love you" upon and carry home to our mothers.

6

Previous studies have shown that astronauts are exposed to a range of health issues when taking prolonged trips into space, including losses in bone density and muscle mass and vision anomalies, but now it's been shown that there is more to be concerned about than those problems. The rounder the heart becomes, the weaker it gets. A rounded heart is a heart at risk.

7

Once, riding in her car while I was visiting Maine, I listened to my host tell a story about hitting a moose on the stretch of highway we were traveling. A family had pulled up behind her on the shoulder, the father asking, "You got a use for that moose?" I smiled, thinking that was the punch line, but there was more. A moment later she described the haunch of moose she'd bartered from that family. "That moose was all mine, by rights," she said, "but the father dressed it out, so it was a fair trade." Even though it was raining heavily, she accelerated, our speed feeling like an exclamation point, the air inside the car so rich with story, change easily entered me. Because I love to eat organ meat, I asked her whether she'd received part of the heart and liver. "Not the heart," she said. "Not that."

8

And last week, in Pennsylvania, when my vocabulary for encouragement stumbled and stalled, I offered my sister the weak consolation of listening to her analyze the pros and cons of heart surgery. The muscle, she said, can regain what's been lost. Just in case, I've updated my will. Three hours, on average, this operation takes, she went on, though by then I was fixed on the sort of planning that included a will revision, the summary she provided about how post-operative rehab is organized failing to adhere to the moist walls of my memory.

9

Both of us had listened for years to our father's reports on his aging heart. About the tempo at first, the pacemaker fresh under his skin after he'd fainted at the wheel and drifted, through luck, into a field as level as his crab-grassed lawn. Sixty, he'd say, as if he was in training. The first time he exposed its shape near his shoulder I imagined his body penetrated by some circular alien who would, inevitably, invade his blood.

10

After our class had inspected the cow's heart, Miss Hutchings unwrapped the hearts of chickens and turkeys, the hearts of swine and sheep. She arranged them by size on the thick, brown paper sack, leaving a space, we knew, for ours. Richard Heckman, whose father's heart had halted, examined his hands. Anne Cole, whose father had revived to cut hair at the mall, stepped back, turning away from the entry to the steer's aorta, the four chambers we were required to know.

11

A long-held belief of many traditional cultures is that eating the organs from a healthy animal supports the organs of the eater. For example, eating the brains of a healthy animal improves clear thinking, and eating animal kidneys will cure people suffering from urinary disease. That logic means that the best way of treating a person with a weak heart is to feed the person the heart of a healthy animal. There are countless reports about the success of these types of traditional practices. None of them have been verified by scientific testing.

12

"Feel this," my father said, guiding my hand to the simple braille of his new pacemaker. "Sixty," he said, "over and over like a clock." I told him about the billion heartbeats of the mammal, how the shrew had three years to live at 800 beats per minute, and the cat had twelve at 200. "We have thirty years," I said, "because we use up 100,000 beats per day, but we get more because of science and medicine and help from how slowly we mature." When I told him this, my father was well over eighty, closing in on three billion, and I was past two billion.

13

Some statistics I didn't tell my father:

The human heart usually weighs about ten ounces, but the heart of the blue whale often weighs about 1300 pounds. It averages about 8-10 beats per minute that can be heard two miles away. On the other hand, the tiny hearts of hummingbirds are the largest proportionate to their minuscule body weight. Their heart rate runs to over 1000 beats per minute when they're active, but it slows when they sleep to less than 100, a necessity, or they would starve to death before morning.

14

According to the Alaska Department of Fish and Game, the average weight of a moose heart is three pounds. "It's like holding a football," the spokesman adds.

15

"The heart doesn't work as hard in space, which can cause a loss of muscle mass," says the lead scientist for ultrasound at NASA and senior author of the study of astronauts' hearts. Though the astronauts' hearts returned to their normal, more oval shape, shortly after their return to Earth, what's left to learn is whether there are serious, long-term consequences, something that can't be known for years.

16

"You know these things when you teach in a medical school," she says. "I've known for quite some time my heart cannot heal itself." She talks as if I, too, have always known she's had what she calls a "persistent disability," something "nagging whose voice has gotten louder." As if that voice could carry hundreds of miles, revealing her heart's distress. She says the surgery is a choice that's been made by her body.

She is thin. Skeletal comes to mind, and all I can think to say is, "It's good you have the inside information on your surgeon."

"I'm thankful that I know these people," she says. "I trust them."

17

Until I was twelve years old, I looked forward to the ritual of tiny candy hearts being shared at the Valentine's Day parties we had in grade school. *Love You Much*, it said in blue letters on the pink candy. *Be Mine* was repeated in red letters on pale blue hearts. From fourth to sixth grade, I looked at Susanna Frank or Nancy Harris or Kathy McMichaels each time I swallowed one, sending sign language their way.

18

The ultrasound pictures of the long-term-in-space astronauts' hearts are stunning. The hearts look as if they've been molded like clay, becoming so nearly circular they appear to be incapable of working. It doesn't surprise me to learn that astronauts often get lightheaded and faint upon standing when they return to earth because of a sudden drop in blood pressure. I think of my father, hospitalized at last, admitting he had, despite the pacemaker, fainted twice when standing, the third time after bending to place his ball on a tee at a public golf course. Despite my father's protests, his friend had called an ambulance. Within a week he underwent his second heart repair, this time triple bypass surgery.

19

The day after we looked at animal hearts, Miss Hutchings asked us to take our pulses. Using the stethoscopes she'd brought to class, we listened to each other, boy to boy, girl to girl, because of the chance we'd touch. The images of those butcher hearts faded while I dreamed of pressing my ear to the rhythmic hearts of Susan Rolfe and Janelle Frank, whose breasts, so far, had brushed me a few times while dancing. And then Miss Hutchings recited the quart total of our blood, the distance it must travel, leaving and returning. We learned all of the names for the necessary routes it followed, ending with capillaries so close to the surface I understood, though she didn't say it, we could nearly reach them with our lips and tongues, rushing the blood to each of the sensitive sources for joy.

20

The sugar Valentine's candy I once loved in grade school are called "conversation hearts" in the ads for them on the Internet. They come in two vague sizes—small and large—but both kinds still feature the familiar messages from my childhood: *Marry Me, Sweet Talk, Darling*, all of the speaking hearts in pastel colors, three pounds for $15.76.

21

Now there are variations on that candy's simple design:
Heart-shaped Twizzlers
Heart-shaped lollipops
Heart-shaped sucker rings that fit on a finger
Heart-shaped candy strung into bracelets
And colorful, decorated heart-shaped boxes in multiple sizes that contain those heart-shaped candies, the packaging suggesting a truncated Russian doll.

22

A woman named Mercy Brown was once exhumed for public autopsy. The people in the town in which she had lived believed that a current local cluster of consumption might be worsened by those who had died from that disease, but it could be bettered by burning the uncorrupted heart of the victim. Not only might there be an end to an epidemic, there was a chance, people said, that her brother Edwin might be cured of his tuberculosis by eating the ashes of her heart. Mercy's father had to watch his daughter raised from the grave after being months buried. He had to endure the burning of her heart. Edwin, at last, swallowed the ashes, but he died, regardless, in two months, leaving his father to live alone and remember his daughter being twice buried. This happened in Vermont, in 1892. Mercy Brown was also thought by many to be a vampire.

23

The rounding of the heart could mean trouble for people who want to embark on long-term missions to Mars. Astronauts currently spend up to six months at the orbiting International Space Station, which is staffed by rotating crews. Missions to Mars would take about 18 months and may offer no return trip.

24

As if she wants me to be convinced her upcoming operation is routine, my sister tells me our cousin has undergone his third operation, that he has flown from Virginia to a Texas hospital for the latest surgery. So thin, she says, his pants want to fall down, his shirts hang like curtains, reminding me how, every late August, my mother held up what he'd outgrown, what I'd grow into, dressing me for school and church for a year, two if we were lucky, teaching the lesson of the threadbare, the ill-fitting and the out of style, learning what was good enough. He's still standing on his own two feet, my sister says, wearing her hand-me-down language, adding he's in our prayers and he's a fighter like a litany, like I should say amen or sing the Doxology before a recessional hymn of hope. My sister, who learned to sew her own clothes, who wore homemade, but new, who needed to perfect the careful cut and stitch because she was older than every female cousin, declares "Our time will come" like some minister for fatalism. She's at the window of the spare room where I've slept, saying the weather, so sunny and mild, is heavenly while I try to ignore the sewing machine, the half-finished skirt and the thick file of patterns collected in the good light I have to tear my eyes from.

25
Is it safe to eat a fresh raw moose heart?

Someone has already posted that question in an Internet forum about large game animals. He received half a dozen responses:

"I wouldn't. Chances are you will be just fine afterward, but eating that heart raw isn't very smart. As a rule of thumb you shouldn't eat anything raw from a game animal, especially an internal organ like the heart."

"No, it's not safe to eat the raw flesh of a moose or a deer or any wild animal, you can get heart worm."

"Apparently you forgot why we let large game animals hang after we gut them and then let the carcass chill to near 32 degrees. It's to kill the intramuscular parasites."

26

Now it is understood that in order to keep the heart healthy in space, astronauts must know the amount and type of exercise they need to perform to guarantee their safety on prolonged spaceflights. It's been suggested that exercise regimens developed for astronauts could also help people on Earth who have physical limitations also maintain good heart health. Those models could also give doctors a better understanding of common cardiovascular conditions for ground-based patients.

27

During the last years of his life, approaching ninety, our father wore sweaters even in summer, so cold, so often, he kept the windows shut in his un-air-conditioned house. He would probe for his pulse, reporting, "Still there." After that small, brief joke, he'd wait five minutes, sometimes ten, before listening to his wrist again, head bowed, leaning forward, as if he needed to coax a heartbeat with prayer.

28

When I attended my 50th high school class reunion recently, there was a large poster that was labeled "In Memoriam." It listed those from my class who had died, a bit reminiscent of the Vietnam Memorial, complete with a few small, impulse tributes of programs and table favors laid beneath it. Susan Rolfe and Janelle Frank, I discovered, had each been dead for more than twenty years. Except for our war dead, causes weren't listed, but like all the others, their hearts had stopped.

29

In the midst of writing this essay, I take a heart age test and learn my heart is a year younger than my age but I have a 22% higher risk than average to have problems in the next ten years. I remind myself that I've lowballed all of my answers, that this is a worst-case scenario, but there's no denying my mother's heart failure when she was younger than I am, my father's bypass and pacemaker, my sister's impending open heart surgery.

30

A few answers to the raw moose heart question were more condescending:

There is an Animal Planet RV show about humans getting animal parasites. You stand a good chance of being their next guest star.

If you want to take the chance, it's your body.

31

Everything points to a glass or two of red wine being heart-helpful, but I drink only white wine and then only rarely, preferring beer. There is evidence that hearty laughter is good for the heart, but I seldom laugh out loud. I blame it on my family history, all those dour, judgmental Germans drinking beer and frowning until they tumbled with heart attacks and strokes.

32

There seems little question that eating organ meats has fallen out of favor among people I know. I tell them that liver, kidney, and heart are some of the most nutrient-rich foods you can eat, but there aren't any takers. At the grocery store, when I look for veal or lamb kidneys, there are none, and when I settle for a package of chicken hearts, the clerk goes "Eeew!" and acts as if she'll pass it through without ringing it up just to avoid touching it.

33

Even when, in the assisted living home, my father stopped watching television, when he slept twelve hours a day and napped three times, his fingers went to his wrist as he woke, repeating, "Still there," even when he gave in to the wheelchair. Even when half his weight vanished although he ate, like always, everything that was served, even when his sentences turned shorter, the ends lost like addresses, phone numbers, and the names of the dead, his fingers returned to his wrist to read the braille for "still there," while I waited, despite reason, holding my breath for his up-to-the-minute news.

34

Although raw moose heart is uniformly cautioned against, there are several methods posted on the Internet for how to prepare moose heart for cooking, most of the directions similar to this:

When the heart is still fresh, soak it in a bucket of cold sea water or fresh water to flush out the blood. Rinse well. Trim the fat and the tops of the valves off well so that the final product is mostly red and the top is relatively level, with clear access to the chambers of the heart. At this point, the heart can be kept in the freezer if wrapped well in saran wrap and butcher paper, however it is best when eaten fresh.

The recipe calls for:
1 moose heart
½ loaf of your favorite white bread
About 4 stalks of celery, chopped into small pieces
1 onion, chopped
2 cloves garlic, minced
2 T parsley leaves
2 t rosemary
2 t oregano
1 t sage
olive oil
3 T butter
salt to taste
pepper to taste
water, red wine, soy sauce to taste

35

This morning, the day of my sister's surgery, a waitress spread whipped cream into a thick, valentine heart across my son's banana-walnut pancakes. Because, she said, a circle would never make you think it's a heart, so unashamed of sentiment, her heavy body turned delicate in the sweetened air.

36

All this afternoon I regret the impossibility of omniscience. And yet I am thankful. At last, from across the room, my wife's phone sings its song of incoming text. And though the news, this time, is good, in the altered atmosphere, I believe our dependable, dangerous hearts are becoming spheres.

THE SIMPLE SIMILE FOR MEDICINE

1

Once a month, on Sunday evening after church, the sorrows kept the women in the kitchen. My cousins and their mother. My grandmother. My aunt and my mother, all of them foraging through the nerves for pain.

They sighed and rustled until one of them would name her sorrows, a cue for sympathy's murmurs and the first offering of possible cures: three eggs for chills and fever, the benefits of mint and pepper, boneset, sage, and crocus tea. Nothing they needed came over-the-counter or through prescriptions because those remedies didn't bear a promise from the God who blessed the recipes handed down from the lost villages of Germany. For the great aunt with dizzy spells. For the second cousin with the steady pain of private swelling. For passed blood, for discharge and the sweet streak from the shoulder.

In the pantry, among pickled beets and stewed tomatoes, there were jars of dark, honeyed liquids, vinegar and molasses sipped from tablespoons for sorrows so regular the women spoke of them as if each pain were laundry to be smoothed by the great iron of faith which set creases worthy of paradise.

From across the shadowed room and through the doorway, they might have been speaking from clouds like the dead. What mattered when the room went dark was the voices reaching into the lamp-lit living room of men who listened, then, looking past each other and nodding at the nostrums offered by the tongues of the unseen.

2

My father insisted the name of God was work, half or more of each day but Sunday. On Saturdays, from seven to midnight, he played cards, and then he said goodbye and slept until Sunday School, church, and the long, white-shirted wait until Sunday dinner: stuffed pie shells and sweet green peppers, filled tomato halves and cabbage leaves. So pretty those meals were, yet economical, and on our table, the Sundays we didn't spend at my grandmother's, were decorative dinners prepared the night before: the shimmering, shaped Jellos; the rank and file of peeled and slivered apples.

My father could count the waste on food. "More," he said. "There's more," pointing out kernels of corn on the cob, melon on the rind, meat along a greasy bone. He showed me how nothing I needed should get trimmed with fat, repeated the lesson of the breed of caterpillars who feed precisely on the leaves they're born to, keeping the edges smooth, nothing ragged or leftover to attract the birds who see the carelessness of the unfinished from a distance. Crusts of bread, cold peas, potato skins—I learned each waste was sin, that an angry sky was waiting to fall upon me with beak and claws.

Yearly, at Christmas, my mother baked a set of designs into anise cookies from which, if I chose carefully, I could recreate the manger scene, complete with Magi. For Easter, she browned crosses into sweet rolls. And for every ordinary Sunday, before she cooked, she arranged flowers on the altar to remind us of the church's shut-ins.

They signified sorrows that ended with death: chrysanthemums for the crippled; asters for the crazed; lilies for the ones so aged they had taken permanently to bed as if weighed down by names as shut-in as the past: Esther and Maude, Florence and Pearl Mae; Amos and Zachariah, Otto, Laird.

The church was full of rumors of lumbago, stories of neuritis, neuralgia, and the strange neurasthenia of hysterical spinsters. All of the shut-ins suffered and were buried, entering the threats and promises of the Apostles' Creed, leaving behind the mysterious fear of the out-of-doors, the sudden shakes, the palsies, and the eyes refusing daylight.

A year after my mother died, my father wove pine boughs while I waited at his kitchen table, and then he called out the passing of each mile to thirteen, the right turn through the open gates to her plot in the Garden of Dreams. He laid those evergreen crosses by the headstone of my mother and the four nearest relatives in a symmetry of remembrance, and then he removed what he'd left for the eleventh-month anniversary, adding those branches to the full plot's border of woven designs so they could extend the decorative work of God.

3

Our family doctor declared measles the most contagious of any disease, saying nothing about jealousy, greed, and the rest of the seven deadly sins whose figures I'd colored in Sunday school. One week it was the fat face of sloth, another the mole-plagued mirror for envy or lust covered by a thousand pock marks as if it caused a terrible rash.

My mother, for my first fourteen years, trusted that doctor who, twenty-five years earlier, had scarred her thigh with a silver-dollar-sized vaccination. He made house calls; he'd delivered her at home and kept her from diphtheria and smallpox and the complications of infections. She stored his medicines until I caught what my sister had suffered years before: Ear drops. Penicillin. Antibiotic creams. They aged like the interest on money saved, and more where that came from if we scrubbed our hands with hot water before we prayed one after the other and sat up straight to clean our plates.

"God's medicine," she said, meaning obedience, and she was right or as lucky as that doctor who thought he understood the simplest cure of childhood, taking out my tonsils to ease my earaches so frequent I thought their pain a common curse, that they would disappear like baby teeth and bring me the good fairy's overnight of profit when I put my memorized faith in the anesthesia of what I didn't know.

4

When my mother talked about sickness, she named the foreign diseases she was certain we would not get: Elephantiasis. Yellow fever. Cholera. Yaws. "Such places," she said, meaning their sources, and I have never traveled to one of those countries where the world's worst maladies seem to begin, slaughtering thousands before experts arrive to track the index case. I've never entered a jungle where men bleed from their pores or women swell into monstrous clouds. I've stayed at home and seen no one die but one fat man dropped suddenly to a noon street corner across from me and a coworker who knew CPR and used it fruitlessly on his chest and mouth.

For years, when I talked about sickness, I mentioned my mother and her sister and the rest of my family who slipped silently to death. I meant their shattered hearts or the sudden lightning of massive stroke. I meant the two times I'd been wired for walking the treadmill for the EKG before I listened apprehensively to my pleasant doctor.

When my wife mentioned sickness, she named the hidden tumors of her family, including the suspected threats to brain, kidney, and bone for which she'd been scanned, the symptoms which drove her to a series of photographed reports.

Still negative, we learned each time, left to think of the worst diseases we'd really had, pneumonia and rheumatic fever, guessing our odds in the outbacks of self-treatment. I thought of the amplifiers of alcohol and greasy food. I thought of driving's bad habits and refusals to change. We shared a few drinks, and I recited the place names for the newest ways the body can be entered: Ebola. Lassa. Marburg. Machupo. Such clumsy misdirection, but they sounded like a roster of devils. No, they sounded like the angels of faithlessness who manifest themselves to the healthy.

5

The summer my grandmother and my aunt died, I learned about the doctor who cured patients by long-distance, sending sickness to limbo through the power of belief. Thousands, he said he saved, from far away, and those who couldn't call sent writing samples, clues enough for that doctor to heal by. He didn't claim he could do miracles for the mute, which was what I needed the afternoon I failed the buddy system of the church camp pool because I followed the wall to fourteen feet to pretend I could push off to the backstroke of buoyant faith.

Reach and pull, I said to myself as I posed. Reach and pull, I repeated, strokes so simple the animals used them. And then, suddenly jostled free of my handhold, I reached back and sank in the stoical splendor of silence.

I touched bottom and rose. I said nothing and reached, sinking again and floundering up a second time to the white inner tube of the lifeguard as if I'd been swimming for hours and cramped, dragged ashore like an exhausted channel crosser.

That Tuesday morning and the remainder of that week I was learning the rewards for faith — health, hope, salvation, and the Bible's great promise that the Balm of Gilead would heal the faithful. Nothing was said by the camp counselors about the way a door-to-door boot polish salesman named Samuel Solomon, over a hundred years earlier, had lifted that name from Christianity's public domain and claimed its second coming a cure for drunkenness, debauchery, the horrors of the mind, and most impressively, a yellow fever epidemic in New York. How that entrepreneur had suspended "God's gold" in solution and completed the other 90% of that popular potion with the distraction of brandy, something like the sugar content of "Salvation's Candy," ten cents for Life–Savior Jesus, "scripture message included," years ago, with that sweet hope, what I bought at the church camp's store an hour after I was saved by the O-ring of the lifeguard.

6

From ninth grade through twelfth grade, my overweight classmates did the dance of pills and chalk-flavored shakes, or else they sat it out with sugar-substitutes. I gobbled and scarfed and never gained a pound. I learned the history of the diet mania, dismissing, all through high school, the lard ass, the porker, the big belly of the slow and sloppy.

Fat was ruin. Fat forced the side effects of chemistry. Fat was the first question when Mr. Buccarelli, during tenth grade, assigned Kafka's "The Hunger Artist" and cited its main character as part of his campaign for the sacred artistry of denial.

Mr. Buccarelli lived close to my house. Because he had one son my age, I knew he ran his three children like dogs and used the leash of his leather belt on their softest parts to free them from sloth. I knew he took no sick days from teaching, missed none of his nights securing the mall.

Mr. Buccarelli adhered to the diet of coffee and cigarettes; he stuffed himself until cancer opened the secrets of his larynx while I matched, during my junior year, the story of my pulse rate to the published numbers of the thin and fit.

I did calisthenics and ran for miles because I wanted to achieve the slow rhythm of world records. I also wanted thick steaks and cheeseburgers, and I meant to fool the starvers with my secret shifts of running distances huge as the timed feats of fraudulent professional fasters like Ann Moore, who claimed six foodless years and beat the witness tests with milk wrung from the towels she washed with. Or Sarah Jacob, who lasted through unverified months, according to her parents, without food and water. Both of them heard applause until they were watched by experts on deceit. Ann Moore confessed, on the ninth day, to the ordinary flaws of thin and weak; Sarah Jacob, however, recanted nothing, rapt with traditional belief until she quietly relinquished breath.

7

"Milktoast," my father said, when I whined about the home remedy of diluted boric acid for athlete's foot, poison ivy, or hives. "Pantywaist," he hissed, calling up the old names for timidity. "Weak is all he was," my father muttered, his voice crackling like a burning bush the evening Jack Swartz, our neighbor, fired a shotgun into his face. He meant Jack Swartz's excessive drinking and rumored liver cancer to be a lesson to me and my own set of fears and weaknesses, and the next afternoon I took a full set of spikes just below my knee at the finish of a track-practice interval because I wouldn't lengthen conditioning's distance by leaving the rail.

"Lucky you," Coach Lange said, meaning I was missing the next six quarter miles because this wasn't a scratch whose possible infection could be called out by elbow grease and the foregone grimace of iodine. These were the punctures that demanded a tetanus shot, and my father drove me to make sure our new doctor was thorough.

"Almost isn't good enough," he'd said three times on the drive to the office, but suddenly, while the doctor injected me, my father looked like someone idling in a sealed garage. "Give me a minute," he said, but the doctor lowered him at once to the level plane of the floor, raising his feet without waiting for directions or uttering soft names like *sissy* I'd been listening to for sixteen years. Six-thirty, dark in March, and my father said "No" to my offer to drive. He stopped on the street of taverns below our house. "For dinner," he said, and he ordered us cheeseburgers and ginger ale. "Look all you want," he said, waving his glass toward so many strangers I might have blacked out in our Chevy, slumped on the seat for a hundred miles.

8

Once I'd read about the coincidence of swine flu shots and sudden death, why had I thought it sensible to volunteer for a dose? And the forms which waived my rights — who would sign such things in the crowded ward of drafted doctors where I stopped and smiled my sorrow at the nurse before I slumped between lines at the government clinic?

I had diplomas from three colleges. I was from Pittsburgh, where two people had died, perhaps, from inoculation, although where I lived that year were mucklands, the great flat acres of onion farmers who tested their earth with weight increments to see if it would hold machinery.

This wasn't the quicksand of Tarzan films, some evil poacher sinking with his load of tusks, but that spring I'd driven to see the slow resurrection of a tractor sunk by a driver who'd been forced to wade to the long embarrassment of safety.

A thousand watchers, looking for the first sign of the buried tractor, fixed on the cables that quivered from the muck. Nothing died this way, I thought, and yet that tractor reared up like a recurring dream. "Should've known better," somebody in the crowd declared, and I agreed with him and the doctor, in November, who ordered me burgers and fries and returned three times, each visit to where I recovered, out of sight, filled with the advice about the consequences of drinking late the night before, skipping breakfast and lunch that day, how prudence protects us, the shot I'd received the right thing despite the strange, miserable luck of the dead.

9

For health, once, for longevity, some people drank wine or warm water to loosen the scum in the sinks of their stomachs. And then they swallowed something called the stomach brush, inch by inch, using liquor to relax the gag reflex.

With something as intrusive as a brush, they kept it down or else. The doctor scrubbed. He plunged and scraped, and then it was withdrawn at last, until the following week, the walls of the stomach invisibly sparkling, its drains opened and cleaned.

Primitive plumbing, all right, or the simple simile for medicine, but nothing I've laughed at, for forty years, from time-to-time bent over sinks to vomit the dregs of fast food and beer.

I've watched that poison swirl dozens of times toward the pause of the elbow joint, tucked my rotten mouth under a strange faucet for a makeshift rinse, thinking, each time, I was about to be cleansed by the medicinal dose of education, all those years on book-a-day to keep one sort of quackery away.

I've lengthened my researched list for foolishness to include the supposed miracle rinse of sea water and the health advantages of tap water transformed by radon ball. But I might as well be swallowing cheap crusts of words, cleaning my plate before taking the stomach brush of self-righteousness.

For nearly ten years the natural brush of my hiatal hernia has swirled up the acids of every hour-old bite, recalling the thick fat of bargain meat, the sulfites and dyes that invite the scrub of surgery. I paint with antacids, double-coat, just in case, everything I swallow. Like the smiling ministers of television, those who understand the close-up; like the way, last month, I brought up so much blood I took my second upper gastro-intestinal exam of the decade and received the score of "significantly changed."

10

When my uncle had cancer of the esophagus, he stopped eating, choosing to fast rather than submit to the mush and liquids my aunt would bring him. At a picnic, six weeks before he died, he sat across from me and ate a hot dog in thirty terrible bites, chewing and chewing, refusing to be helped away from the table until he'd swallowed every soggy bit.

"His sins have been visited upon him," my mother said. My aunt didn't own a blender. For all I know, my uncle refused to allow one in the house. He might have been terrified by the moans of processing everything into soup. Decades later, I could tell him there are ways to vary consistency. Eleven buttons on the one I use; any amount of time I choose to let the blades spin. Chop, twenty seconds. Puree, fifteen seconds. Grind, forty-five seconds. Whip, one minute. Liquefy, no limit.

The Blender Chef. I could restock the ancient, dark shelves of my grandmother. I could slip into the kitchen with the women and murmur my expertise on the body's failures while they evaluated the weight of my sorrow, how likely it was that I'd risk the eternal wrath of God by refusing the simple nostrum of food.

11

The year of the Swine Flu fiasco, in Africa, doctors were recording sudden aches and fevers, bleeding gums, nausea, and odd vomit filled with black, digested blood. There were nuns and nurses dying. There were physicians fleeing like the Yambuku villagers who thought this virus began in the wrath of terrible demons.

And when specialists arrived, when they landed near the Ebola, where the living washed the dead, wiping blood by hand, they worked back to bodies scrubbed by the hands of the dead who had bathed those who had already died, purifying them for the afterlife.

When she watched the news, my mother repeated the fresh names for horror. She fretted over my small children and reminded them of the good medical fortune of where they lived. "We become what we make of ourselves," my mother said. "You won't get such things if you take care," including me in her collective pronoun for judgment.

And those disease experts, before long, were flying to Tanzania where men and women died like infants, thin and small and wracked by diarrhea until they were similes for "the slim," dying from AIDS far from the terrible anger of the God of Sodom.

Panicked, they bought pesticides to swallow, so many, so fast, the village stores ran out, restocked, and ran out again, leaving them to lesions and tumors.

Those scientists retraced, from Tanzania to Uganda, the history of a bolt of material that became known as the Juliana Cloth because that name was so wondrously woven through it that women, with nothing else to barter for fashion, paid the trader with their bodies. All of them had died, the women who loved that cloth, Juliana's stitched name spooling back with those dead, leading science to the dark country of resignation where even the unborn drifted toward the loving hands of the unknowing who wove their inevitable names.

MARKING THE BODY

My doctor, a woman, knows how shyness shrinks men gone vulnerable in the groin. She waits while they unbutton or unzip, turns from me this morning, giving me time to excuse myself with a just-learned story about how, behind a curtain, women would mark a female doll exactly where they hurt, using charcoal to scratch an X on the breasts or the belly or high up on the thighs. My doctor tells me she knows that history. She says my male doll has Xs over the lungs, cross-hatches on the throat, skipping the spot for this morning's mark, the way I've never been so slow to undress for her instruments.

My doctor, who knows when eternity begins to form far out in the future's ocean, covers her hands in the latex of discretion, reaches for me, and says, "The feet of those behind the draperies were bound." My doctor, who would have passed that Barbie to the discreet hands of a physician, examines me as if I were a familiar doll. She breathes high on my naked thighs, that air the first that has failed to stir the stiffening blood.

After she inserts a finger and withdraws it. After she pivots, strips her gloves, and I follow the intimate lines of her breasts and hips to the softness of myself in the last moment when I am wondering what's arriving, she murmurs, "Nice and small," uttering the paradox of the healthy groin.

THE DARKNESS CALL

1

Between our upstairs bedroom and the nearest window of our neighbors, across the arm's length of the space between our second floor rentals, my father, during the last month of my mother's pregnancy with me, strung a clutch of cans. He worked nights, and he needed to know, in case of emergency, my mother had a way to make a darkness call. He counted on our neighbors, a minister and his wife, to be sober, something he didn't expect from the couple downstairs, both of them drinkers. Moreover, those church people had the only phone and the only car on our block.

My father worked in a bakery located an uphill mile away. In July, 1945, the minister's wife woke from sleep to the rattle of cans, called the bakery, and helped my mother down the stairs. I was ready to be born, about to open my eyes on the great flash of the A-bomb from Socorro. I was about to hear my father sing the miracle of his brothers all safely home and to learn war could be won by brains.

Birth was a cord of rattling cans. In every picture of the first astonishing cloud over New Mexico, my mother clutches that string and knows my father will take six minutes and thirty seconds to reach where she pants in the pastor's car, waits for him to grow large and white, his apron twisted sideways like a shredding sail.

2

"Play *Nuclear War*, a fast-paced comical card game for 2-6 players of all ages."

If I weren't standing in the historical museum in Los Alamos, I would think somebody is making this up, but there's more to this display. For instance, *Up an Atom*, which, according to the copy on the box, I could learn to play in fifteen minutes.

There are dozens of such curiosities: A picture of an Atomic Cake from *Time Magazine*, tiny models of battleships floating on blue icing under a mushroom cloud concocted of whipped cream. An Atom Bonnet shaped like the familiar mushroom worn by a woman in a Los Alamos Easter Parade.

And then I'm happy to see a placard that explains how women, earlier in the century, had fainted on the way up, frightened to blackouts by the cliff when they came to visit their sons at the Los Alamos Ranch School, a sort of year-round Boy Scout camp for the very rich. Driving up the mountain to Los Alamos an hour before, I'd regretted my date of birth and the decades of associations that had driven me to seek out a belated anniversary for myself and the atomic bomb. A sheer drop formed a few feet to the right of our rental car, and when the road narrowed to two lanes near the top of the mesa, a line of impatient horn blowers had formed behind my pace of twenty-five miles per hour.

My wife sees my joy. "Those women weren't on a paved road," Liz reminds me. "Most of them were relying on the surefootedness of horses and the handling of men," and I follow the list of alumni from Bill Veeck to Gore Vidal before I pass on to the Bikini bomb test exhibit, the first displayed photographs taken after my birth.

Operation Crossroads, the display says, and I learn at once that, after Nagasaki, no other bombs were detonated until the United States set off two more in July, 1946. "To scare the shit out of the rest of the world," a thin, stooped man says from my left. He moves closer to me, dragging a bottle of oxygen, his breath hissing like an aged Darth

Vader's. While I give him a minute to settle, I read about the plans for a scuba diving resort that will make use of the scuttled fleet of target ships, how tourism might bring somebody back to an area contaminated by years of atomic testing.

"You know," the old man says, "they shut down my Van de Graaf Generator, and then they confiscated the physics books at the college where I taught in Florida. And they cut out the pictures from the journals. Imagine sending people to all those libraries."

"I was born almost to the day of the first test," I say.

He hisses three times, long enough for me to think I've been stupid to say it. Finally, he asks, "Your father an educated man?"

"No," I say, and he relaxes.

"Well, he didn't know what he was getting you in for then, most likely."

3

The way down is a lot easier because the car is in the lane nearest the uphill cliff. I don't worry about swerving into a wall of rock, become so confident I look for a spot to pull off for pictures. Even Liz, who would rather be shopping in Santa Fe, appreciates the choice of sites to develop the bomb. "It was meant to be inaccessible," she says. "If you were a spy, you'd have a hard time leaving without being noticed."

"And yet somebody did," I say when I park and walk at once to the edge, trusting my feet more than the rental car. "I remember the first Russian A-bomb test. It's one of the first memories I have. 1949, the year my Great-Uncle Willy bought the first television in our family, and my father bought our first refrigerator."

We watched The Goldbergs and Mama and The Life of Riley on my uncle's blonde Magnavox when we visited on Friday nights. My mother peeled apples for coffee cakes my father would bake while we were asleep. Except for Jackie Gleason, and then William Bendix, it seemed as if all the men on night-time television had accents. Soon enough, an actor on The Goldbergs was fired because he was suspected of having

54

Communist sympathies. No matter what the precautions, the A-bomb secrets had reached the Soviets. Their first bomb was a duplicate of Fat Man, the one the United States had dropped on Nagasaki.

4

The day before, in Santa Fe, Liz had dragged me into an old church that charged admission to see its "miraculous staircase." Inside, the double helix of the stairs spiraled behind barriers so tourists wouldn't test it after they'd been told it should collapse, according to some architects, when climbed. I thought of the huge ants of M.C. Escher crawling up and down to emphasize the optical illusion of those stairs turning inside out and upside down as they searched for an end to the trick of architecture.

We listened to the piped in voice of the church claim a carpenter traveled by donkey to tell the nuns he would build them the staircase they needed to reach the inaccessible choir loft. After another glance, I sat in a pew and watched my wife take pictures. In front of me were three women who knelt and signed themselves, and two men wearing headphones that were telling them to look left, then right, then up and behind them.

According to the free public voice, the carpenter had built the staircase and disappeared without accepting payment or providing railings. On the morning of the nuns' first climb, they cautiously crept upward to sing. And then, faced with descent on those coils, they hesitated, then froze on the upper loop until, one by one, they dropped to hands and knees to crawl that spiral back to earth.

5

By second grade, the threat of Soviet A-bombs targeted to Pittsburgh, the steel mill capital of the world, sent us into biweekly bomb drills. My family moved three miles farther from Pittsburgh, but a year later everybody in my new grade school practiced hugging the basement walls to save ourselves from the A-bomb. I thought my new teacher looked old enough to die even if nothing fell from the Pittsburgh sky. She had grayer hair than my grandmother who was already dead. She could have been on my Sunday school program cradling children in her arms and repeating old women's prayers against flood and fire.

Later, we climbed the cement stairs, filed through the halls, and refilled the classrooms like water. The next plane made me foresee the first tumbling bomb while my classmates were singing "America" as if it were something besides curriculum.

That summer McCarthy repeated himself to the army on television, and I was sitting against a friend's game room wall when I heard his father say, "Fuck you" to the screen. I looked to see what was so terrible it made him outraged, but there were just men talking. He took us downstairs. He showed us bottled water, the cans of Spam, and the radio that marked all the frequencies for woe. "You listen to this," he said, and I heard the noise of a construction site: jackhammers, heavy machinery, the whisper of passing cars.

There were spiders on the walls; there was a shell so dry in a giant, corner web, I tried to figure what flavor it might have been. I stared at the cinderblock. He'd painted it light blue because it said comfort, what they'd need, maybe, for years, his work aligned with half-life. In September, my old teacher's permed hair looked blue under the school's new fluorescent lights. She laughed about the effect of radiation on gray when I asked her how it turned that way.

6

We spend two days in Zion National Park, marvel at the landscape, but I've bought a book called *American Ground Zero*, and the names of nearby places on the map are so frequent that when we leave the park I understand we're in "cancer alley," a series of towns — Washington, St. George, Cedar City — mentioned in Carole Gallagher's locations for leukemia epidemics in the 1950s and 1960s.

Soon, most of the people we meet tell us at once they are Mormons, and they are so upbeat and calm they seem to be residents of the fictional town of Stepford. As soon as we give them an opening, they talk about the promise of eternity, how the only point to earthly life is to prepare for heaven. I can see how they make a population that will take things without complaint. "The best is yet to come" is a credo a secretive government would want the dying young to believe.

Liz and I discuss turning into Nevada, driving into the wastelands we recognize from reading *American Ground Zero*. We should see Yucca Flats and Frenchman's Flats for ourselves, but after a few miles we begin to extrapolate the hundreds of miles of moonscape. "A great place to bury used razorblades," was one of the images the military had employed to convince the government to create test sites here, and we acquiesce to the description, citing time and feeling cheap and guilty all the way to Salt Lake City where we walk among thousands of smiling Mormons, touring their showpiece worship sites and finding a plaque that tells us, incredibly, that Joseph Smith saw his vision along the Susquehanna River, which we can see from our upstairs windows.

"Which part of the river?" I ask a woman, and she tells us the whole story, crossing the country with the faithful pioneers instead of pinpointing the spot on the Susquehanna. I try to interrupt her, but she prattles on, ecstatic to be reciting her memorized speech. As the Mormons get closer to Salt Lake, I back away, but she is busy reading off some internal cue card, and before long I'm fifty feet away and can watch her speak to the space just to the left of Liz's shoulder, a mid-point she'd established while I was still nearby.

7

"Cloudshine," a general called radiation, to put a pleasant spin on the cloud's pink glow. Another expert hypothesized the theory of hormesis, claiming that long-term, low-level exposure to radiation would toughen people up toward longer lives. "Pantywaist," he might have been saying, "sissy, mama's boy," the names my father and his military veteran brothers called me if I whined in the years just before and after I entered high school when they were examining me for signs of proper manhood.

In October of 1962, my relatives gathered after church on Sunday. My father and his brothers turned on the radio, and their white shirts spoke answers to the questions that hollered from the console. Would Khruschev launch? Would Kennedy bluff us dead?

There was a pilot, a tail-gunner, and an infantryman in those chairs: Korea, Germany, North Africa. One uncle knew the weight of the A-bomb, the exact radius of readiness. One aunt shoved cloves into a brown-sugared ham; one brought green tumblers of root beer and shook her head as if she knew her husband's cancer-before-his-time was tracing the great arc of the ballistic missile. "You build them, you use them," her husband said.

A toy football lurched off my lap and rocked three seconds of silence through the living room. It lay quietly through the pilot's tale of the secret plan for bats, how hundreds were dropped, carrying napalm, from a plane to test one more way to destroy Japan. It didn't matter, he said, that the bombs were too heavy, because most of those bats, as usual, were sleeping, and tumbled to earth like humans.

The radio switched to music. That uncle said survivors flew to the nearest available caves and burned the airport's hangars. He picked up the football and added, "That plan was scrapped in May of 1943, and then they handed the war over to the scientists." He tossed that rubber ball at the brother who'd lifted and landed an A-bomb while an aunt shouted, "Ready" so loudly she might have intended to summon the family next door to dinner.

8

When we get to Moab, the atomic history tour I've mapped nearly over, we seek out the local history of uranium. The town has a museum as well, much of it devoted to movies which used its rugged landscape to show desolation and solitude.

I've seen nearly all of the movies. *The Comancheros*, for instance, which I watched in high school, John Wayne and Lee Marvin in a western which carelessly showed power lines and contrails in some of its scenes. *The Greatest Story Ever Told*, the land around Moab doing its body double for the wilderness where Jesus spent forty days.

A more recent film is *Space Hunter*, the 3-D science fiction movie from the 1980s, Moab, by now, the landscape of a desolate planet, but I'm there for the uranium, pictures of miners and the inadequate equipment they wore. Nearby is a display of related products: Radium Vitalizer Water — "The more you drink the better we will like it," the ad copy cheerily exclaims.

There are more slogans to remember, among them the straightforward

"Drink radioactive water."

"Who could be so silly?" Liz says, sounding ominously like my mother. "Don't be silly," she said to me so many times I looked it up, once, and discovered its origins and changes. It was derived from *selig*, which meant *holy* and then *innocent* and then *gullible*, sliding downhill to *foolish in faith*. So silly it is, I think — the great silliness of Radithor, a potion men drank for sexual prowess. Or radioactive soap, marketed in 1918, the year my father was born and another war ended, with the slogan "Glow with vitality and health."

But silly, suddenly, seems too easy an explanation. After all, thousands of men, looking for work, were convinced to enter the nearby uranium mines without sufficient protection. We leave the museum to conduct our own tour of a uranium mine. Long closed, the entrance set high on a hillside reachable only by a road so narrow and steep we know we must climb on foot. The mine, blocked by rubble, is a disappointment, and Liz reminds me of invisible horrors, more reasons for inaccessibility.

In Sunday school, shortly after the resolution of the Cuban Missile Crisis, a man who sold insurance during the week explained another newly-touted benefit of uranium, that it pulled diseases from the body, how patients entered played-out uranium mines as if they could be cured in radioactive caves. "Their faith is misguided," he said, citing a man named Elisha Perkins, who once held a patent on "the tractor," two rods which drew diseases from the body by a special alignment of alloys. "He thought he was Christ," the teacher said. "Is it any wonder he failed?"

We eat dinner, hours later, in a restaurant located in the former house of the uranium king of Moab. The rooms are full of pictures of Charlie Steen and his cronies, laminated newspaper stories of financial and political success. "He made himself a bundle," our waitress says. "He knew everybody there was to know for a while and then he was gone with the wind."

Which seems appropriate — the wind had brought heavy doses of cloudshine to the people of Utah, the wind had carried a series of smaller doses across nearly every square mile of the United States, including the spots in Pennsylvania and New York where my wife and I and all of our classmates began to laugh about the "duck and cover" civil defense exercises, the waste of time and energy put in by our neighbors who constructed bomb shelters in their back yards.

9

Our last morning in Moab I wake Liz in the five a.m. dark so we can drive to Arches National Park before sunrise. We climb over rocks and scramble up to where we can take pictures of the sunrise through one of the arches. Still early, we are free for a few minutes to sit on an enormous stone and lapse into remembrances: how such land was thought expendable, how the people nearby were considered "a low-use segment of the population."

We'd been to Canyonlands National Park the day before. We'd stopped first at the state park which featured Dead Horse Point, a breathtaking overlook of an enormous, picturesque canyon. None of these rugged and remote national or state parks, unsurprisingly, were formed until after the atomic tests were stopped.

"Look," Liz says, and I stand at once, positioning myself under the arch. She takes two pictures of me and the sunrise, and we quickly trade places. When I peer through the viewfinder, the glare behind her is so suddenly enormous it seems to come from an unfamiliar sun.

SUBSIDENCE, MINE FIRE, THE TOMB OF EVE

My father tells me to turn up Spencer Lane, the first time I've taken this route in thirty years. "Why?" I could ask, but he's sitting up straight so I know I don't have long to wait.

"Look," he says, after we make two right turns. The street is blocked by sawhorses with blinking lights. "Subsidence," he says, "after all these years."

Road Closed is repeated on three signs and I keep driving, allowing him to direct me through a loop of roads to the back side of Stoneridge, the housing plan that covers the hillside near his house. "We can park here and walk without being a nuisance," he says.

He lives less than half a mile away. My friends and I had hiked all over this hillside and the woods just below us until the houses sprang up when I was in high school. "Where were the mines?" I say, and he smiles.

"They started at the bony pile you were afraid of," he says.

"I thought that was a strip mine," I say, recalling the details of my humiliation, how I dropped to my knees on the high, narrow path and said NO to further climbing in front of fifteen Boy Scouts and two leaders, one of which was my father.

"It wasn't big. I don't know where else there were entrances, but it started in Fall Run and ran up through the woods — a hundred years ago, and now it's caving in."

My father had led me back down the narrow trail. He'd walked in front of me without speaking until we reached the road, and nobody, not even the other Boy Scouts, had ever mentioned my failure again.

Now he leads me back toward the sawhorses and the blinking lights to walk the closed streets, and we pass mailboxes tipping toward sunken yards, houses with heavy equipment parked near the shrubbery, a sure sign of cracked foundations. The lights are out in every house; if anyone else is taking the tour, we don't see them.

Fifteen minutes later, my father has me park in front of the fire hall, where a meeting has already begun with township officials and a set of engineering and mining experts. The hall is packed, every chair taken, a triple row of people I imagine are Stoneridge residents jammed along three walls. One by one, twenty-seven in all while we watch, the homeowners walk to the microphone in the center aisle and voice their protests. After each speech, limited, apparently, to two minutes, a round of applause, whether the speaker is loud or soft, profane or polite. And when the first engineer begins to deliver his assurances, my father nudges me toward the door.

"We don't need to hear the rest," he says.

"What's this all about?" I ask as I drive.

"Common cause makes a neighborhood, doesn't it?" he says. "Everybody on those streets was in that fire hall."

"Seems like," I say, the short drive already over.

"It goes way back to 1902. The Glenshaw Coal Company mined the whole area around here."

"I never heard of it."

"And neither did I until all this started."

"All those years when I was hiking those woods, and I never saw an air shaft. Where are they?"

"The closest one I know of is at the end of the street. Back when we had sewers put in, forty years ago now, I thought the Millers were kidding when they said they didn't need to tap in because they dumped their sewage down a mine shaft. I thought they were cheap, but I never did see a sign of a septic tank, none of that telltale rich green you get from having one."

"The mines are that close?" I say. We're back inside the house, and I catch myself listening through my legs for the first sign of the earth shifting.

"Maybe closer."

"How much closer?"

He tells me the township mailed him and the rest of his neighbors a map of the mines in question. If he had bought a lot on the other side of the street, he thinks he would be in danger.

I look at the walls of the living room, expecting to see cracks in the plaster. "The map doesn't tell you for sure?" I say.

"You can look," he says, and I expect the worst.

"It's under the house?"

"I don't think so. The map is hard to read."

He starts to search for the map among stacks of old mail he's piled on the dining room table. I've seen dates on those envelopes running back five years, and I have time to remember the high school where I had my first teaching job and the day the principal asked, over the PA, for everyone in our wing of the building to report to the gym. Depending on their lifestyle, the students thought it was an assembly or a drug bust, but I imagined gas leak or bomb threat, and it turned out none of us was right.

In the field outside the rooms across the hall an enormous sinkhole had suddenly opened, the earth dropping ten feet and forming a crater that spread to within a broad jump of the building.

Mine subsidence, the veteran teachers told me. Everybody knows why the school district got the land so cheap. The crater, measured at 200 feet across, spread no further; the school stayed structurally sound. "We weren't fools when we built it," the contractor said. "We knew where the hollow spots were."

Which is more than my father can say, pretty sure the earth beneath us is solid, but not entirely certain. And my father, who misplaced his bifocals months ago, can't read the map he finally fishes from stack #3.

The tunnels, according to the map, run along the back yards of the houses across the street. Something like that old high school which, more than thirty years later, is still used. Not so lucky are the residents of Stoneridge, a large part of that plan built over a labyrinth of abandoned seams.

"I used to help deliver coal," my father says, and I let him tell me one of his old stories, how, when the truck came, the driver dumped the coal in the alley behind their house. "The basement window was under the back porch," he says. "We had to shovel the coal into bushel baskets, and one of us boys had to get under that porch, take the basket, and hand it down to my father. You didn't want to hear the coal had run out again for a long time after spending a Saturday afternoon under the porch breathing coal dust. We stuffed rags under the cellar door to keep the dust out of the house, so you can imagine the rest."

I remember visiting that house when I was small, how, because my father and his brothers had all moved away, only two rooms took heat from the coal furnace. The registers in the floor of the kitchen and dining room were open; the registers in the living room were closed, the room's two doors shut to smother the draft. And upstairs was a camping trip, heavy quilts and thick comforters because my grandfather only asked his sons to shovel coal once a year.

"It could be worse," I say, and I tell my father about walking through Centralia, the town near where I live that has suffered an underground mine fire for nearly half a century.

He thinks I am making it up, but I show him, on the map of Pennsylvania, the highway that has been closed for years because the fire passed underneath it, causing it to ripple and crack and most likely, if cars and trucks had kept on it, collapse.

The earth is so hot in places you can start paper on fire. Schoolboy stuff, but there are thousands of ruined acres, large stands of dead trees, their roots destroyed by heat. And the town itself, except for a dozen or so diehards, is gone. Literally—the houses razed, the people moved elsewhere because the fire has decades worth of coal left to burn.

"So many mines," my father says at last. "So many things under the ground we don't know what we have down there anymore."

I let him know I agree, but I don't bring up nuclear refuse, toxic medical waste, all of the plastic and such that will outlast us, most likely, by thousands of years.

Those Stoneridge residents who earlier had stood to ask questions were having their fortunes told by old coal, as if millions of years ago the prophecy of compressed, dying plants had foretold their future. Here, coal formed. Here, it did not. The voice of such creation waited nearly an eternity to rise from its seams, and now an answer depended on whether engineers and politicians were willing to drop money into an evening of questions.

So I tell my father the story of the Tomb of Eve, how, for years, pilgrims came to Jeddah, where they believed the Mother of Mankind was living beneath the earth and able to answer their most important questions.

"For a price, of course," my father says, and I nod.

The pilgrims were willing to spend a few coins, no worse than a church offering, and they dropped them into a slot and voiced their queries down the narrow shaft to the holy mother.

"What sorts of questions?" my father asks.

I don't know exactly, but I tell him they were usually questions about dead loved ones or the future. And then I tell him the Mother of Mankind had a personal entrance, that there was more than one tunnel to the warren for secret wants.

"Thirty years it went on," I say, "before she left for good when somebody finally worked his way through the labyrinth."

"Why would anybody believe that was real?" my father says. "As soon as you hear you have to pay, you know it's a racket."

"If it was free, what would you ask?"

My father glances at the map he cannot read before he answers. "What do I pray for, you mean?"

"It doesn't have to be spiritual."

"I'd ask about Ruthy."

"You don't have to tell me," I say, but he rushes on.

"I'd ask her if Ruthy still gets to do the things she loved. Your mother finished the newspaper's crossword puzzle the night she died; she rinsed out her juice glass and put it on the sideboard before she went to bed. For her to be happy she'd have to keep everything tidy. There couldn't be any mess in heaven."

"Maybe there is so she can clean it up forever."

Six months earlier I'd driven back to Pittsburgh to be with him after his quadruple heart bypass, but this afternoon we'd played nine holes of golf before we'd had dinner and driven home through Stoneridge.

"Six or seven years, maybe, this retread will give me," he'd said, using a tone that told me he'd researched the statistics, and I hadn't said anything about how something else could break down, that there was more than one threat under the surfaces of our lives.

All round my father had played best ball of two. Four, he'd recorded after sinking a thirty foot putt on the second try. Five, he'd had me write down after he'd driven his second tee shot down the middle instead of hooking it into the woods. By the ninth hole my father was leading me by a stroke and beaming. While we waited for half of the foursome in front of us to use the drop zone to get over the water, he showed me his scars, the lines and dots of surgery. "The human body can put up wth most anything," he said, and then he topped his first iron and watched it trickle into the pond. A few seconds later he lofted his seven iron onto the near-island of green to put himself into position for another par.

He closed me out by two strokes. I slung his bag over my left shoulder and carried my own over my right, and he walked, to save his spikes and to protect his socks as well, barefoot across the parking lot. My father didn't hurry. He didn't act as if that asphalt was cooking the soles of his feet. "In the sun," he said, "there's a difference between asphalt and concrete," his voice so placid I freed one hand, laid it to the summer surface, and listened, like the deaf, for the music of the earth.

DURING THE FARM SHOW PARADE

In the next town over, early in the parade, the recently acquitted drive their red truck slowly, the Ford F-150 as polished as the fire trucks and the horns of the high school band. From both windows they throw Tootsie Rolls and hard candy wrapped in cellophane to scrambling children, then wave like the mayor and the Farm Show Princess who follow the Civil War re-enactors and their hoop-skirted wives.

An hour ago, because the acquitted said they would carry a sign and a poster, a volunteer had approved their red pickup as a float, slotting it between the Cub Scouts and the Gym Starz in their sparkling tights. Now, all of us along the parade route read the sign that says "Our trial wasted $17,000 of your money" beside a poster of the District Attorney stuffed into a garbage can.

I'm here with my granddaughters, ages six and nine, because I picked a local parade to entertain them. The parade is small, the route short. They live in Los Angeles, have access to the annual Rose Bowl Parade, but here there are farm animals up close and children their age walking by and waving in Brownie uniforms and dance outfits. Both girls are paying attention.

The acquitted, I think, might have passed the victim's family. I concentrate on their mouths to read their words. I watch their gestures for tells.

I'd read the newspaper's daily reports on the trial. Like my neighbors, I'd expected a guilty verdict even though many of the witnesses seemed unreliable. Every adult here must remember the recent testimony about the seventeen year-old fatal beating that was finally being prosecuted. The kegs of beer in the field of a local farm. The large crowd and their heavy drinking. The young man who would be killed coming on to the girlfriend of one of the acquitted, his hand on her bare arm.

All of us likely remember the descriptions of the beating. A half-sister to one of the acquitted saying the victim was "assaulted hard core while people watched." Another witness claiming the victim took a few licks, but "just a little knock around, nobody falling down or like that."

For sure, all of us must remember the farm's owner repeating the advice she claimed to have given the acquitted that day: "You want to kill somebody, you move that body off my property."

Which some claimed they did in the bed of that Ford F-150. Which some asserted they did not. Regardless, every one of those witnesses agreed, that young man's body ended up lying along a seldom used country road. The acquitted, meanwhile, lived as suspects for seventeen years.

My granddaughters love the rabbits in their cages and the tethered calf led by a girl who looks to be about ten years old. I grip their hands to keep them from lunging for the candy, but neither one tugs to free herself, as if the murmur that rises around us as the truck passes is a warning to be wary.

After the acquitted pass, a nearby woman unwraps one of their butterscotch candies. She sucks on it, her mouth working as if she is delivering a curse. I think of how likely it is that some of the spectators are armed. Whether the news of the acquitted's float has reached a relative or close friend of the murdered man.

A man half a block down raises a fist in rage. Or in solidarity. Either way, I'm relieved to see his hand is empty.

One more block and the acquitted turn left, accelerate, and disappear like the immortal.

THE HISTORY OF LIE DETECTION

...to find whether sunshine or cloudiness prevails in the
suspect's mind.
—Hugo Münsterberg, applied psychologist, 1915

1

When a man from a nearby town disappears, leaving his distinctive car behind in a shopping center parking lot, his girlfriend is questioned. The police show so little faith in her answers that she asks to take a lie detector test. After she passes, she speaks to television reporters. "Here," she says, "that settles it," though an investigator suggests the test is unreliable, tainting her with research about how liars beat technology, how those who are truthful can be identified as dishonest.

"God knows what's in my heart," she says, citing the Bible's persistent form of lie detection. "Infallible," she adds, defiantly glancing skyward as if her role in this case can be settled by faith.

2

My father taught the firm handshake, how it tested for the truth of toughness. I needed to master a solid grip unless I wanted to be caught in a weak, effeminate lie.

He taught the truth of exhaustion, the truth of calluses, the truth of

71

scars on the hands, fingernails chipped and black from labor even when the hands were arranged for God, one palm pressed upon the other to receive the body of Christ, who graded each day's worth like a foreman, including how my father, wearing his one white shirt, walked me to where he retrieved our car like a holy valet, my mother and sister waiting in the church doorway like the wealthy.

3

In the early days of lie detection, someone devised the ordeal of the red-hot iron. If no welt appeared when it was applied to the tongue, the suspect was declared not guilty. As if there were a specific number to endure to prove innocence, that glowing iron had to be applied nine times in all to be official.

There was a variant, the ordeal of the red-hot stones. Cross them barefooted without burns and go free. Despite their difficulty, there were ways to beat those tests, working up enough saliva to lessen damage to the tongue, shedding enough sweat to insulate the feet from fire.

Improbable, and yet it was recorded that there were prisoners acquitted, even after the fundamental ordeal of boiling water, the honest arm and hand unscathed after immersion because every god always sides with the innocent.

4

The truth, earlier this morning, was my hands tugging the crown vetch from among the ordered plants whose names I've forgotten while I listed lies I've repeated in order not to be uprooted by the hands of expectation: The lie of public modesty. The lie of daily interest in the accomplishments of others.

When I held my hands, as always, under hot water to scald away the welts I expect from allergies to a host of stems and leaves, I steadied them against the lie of self-sacrifice, then plunged them into the brief ordeal of the sink's hot pool and silently held still.

5

During the early entry of technology into lie detection, the ordeal of balance was invented. To begin, the suspect was weighed precisely by the carved-stone counterweights on an oversize scale. Then he stepped away to listen while the judge, at length, addressed the court as if the mechanical jury were a god. The accused hoped for a long harangue because, as soon as the judge was finished, he had to remount that scale in order to determine whether, during that interval, he had lost weight, what was required to set him free.

6

While the wind lifted grit into our eyes, a man with a telescope showed my wife and me where to look to see elk resting at the base of the volcano. Shadows rushed across the wide runway of obliteration where we paused for photographs, my wife bare-headed, me in a Mt. St. Helen's hat bought minutes before, just after we'd listened to survivors' voices describe mud floods and clouds of ash to corroborate the testimony of the landscape. Finally, I stood on a sample seismograph to make my mark on the unspooling paper, spiking a modest lie with a small, self-conscious leap, then standing still while the graph registered the truth of my pleasure in the misery of others, traveling for hours to sight-see at where hell-to-pay had visited.

7

Finally, science began to examine the possibilities of lie detection, advocating fitting one hand inside a water-filled rubber glove and waiting for a change in blood pressure to determine each nervous lie. At last, science, more reliable, replaced God with Lombroso's Glove because it knew an elevated pulse displaced water, summations the judge needed to learn when he examined evidence presented as a graph, discovering how the body's chemistry sings its mute confession.

8

The summer I was a school janitor, while I cleaned walls with chemicals strong enough to warrant mandatory rubber gloves, my partner, a man named Funovitz who'd worked those walls for thirty years, told the foreman I was the reason why we were behind schedule even though I'd spent hours each day waiting for him to wake from naps and finish reading the morning newspaper, because, he'd said, there was no rush, and I needed to relax.

Now I stood accused, and the foreman gave me a week to straighten up and show him I could do the work. As soon as he left, Funovitz explained that he'd just stood up for me. "You heard me," he said. "I told him right off that we'd catch up."

I didn't see it that way, and when I took off my gloves to scrub my hands before lunch, I inspected my skin as if I expected my damp flesh to show signs of dissolving. Funovitz peeled off his gloves and laid them on the table without washing his hands. "Hey, buddy," he said as we ate our sandwiches and drank from cans of sodas we bought from the vending machine in the cafeteria, "I'll goddamn betcha you're on the job here next week no problem," so at ease I thought he believed every word he said was the truth.

9

Not much is needed to bring a blush into the face of the shamed. A lie, for instance, a denial of guilt, and even the smallest hint of red means blood has shifted suspiciously. It could be measured, Angelo Mosso believed, the blood's giveaway of deceit revealed, and he built, the twentieth century about to begin, a bed so well balanced it would quiver for the smallest lie.

There, in Mosso's Cradle, how stiffly did his subjects lie? As if trip-wired to a bomb, terrified to shiver? The way, in marriage, bodies reveal themselves, so still, yet turning away in the old posture of indifference, a woman and man controlling breath, the untruth of their closed eyes swelling some distant part of them, the ankles and feet expanding with the pooled blood of heart's failure while the dark groin sleeps like a child's immaculate desire.

10

On the Internet, this afternoon, I discover I can subscribe to LiarCard, "the most advanced voice analysis technology for personal use available today." It's advertised for business use, negotiations and hiring, but at the end of the list of possibilities is the one that I'm guessing is most in demand: ". . . to let you know if the person talking with you is not being honest on a specific issue."

Faithfulness, for starters. Love. Even friendship. LiarCard will give me the scoop on anyone's deceit.

There's a toll-free number to call, a PIN number I'll be given by email immediately upon payment. When I click on "sign up," I learn it's $10 for thirty minutes, $80 for 240 minutes, so there's no discount for bulk purchasing. I'm reassured, though, that my minutes won't expire, that if I quickly ferret out the lie I'll be able to come back later when deceit re-enters my life.

All I have to do is make the call and work my way into talking about what matters. Only I can hear the "heartbeat pulse" that plays in the background. Only I can hear the buzz that sounds when the someone I've called may not be telling the truth.

And after I hang up? I can log in and replay that call, listen again to the promises and reassurances I've heard. There are graphs to examine. An analysis to read. Now I know the truth, that how things are said is what reveals us.

Just before I move on, I read the headline promise: "Instantly detects," it says, giving me pause.

11

"Someone in this room is a liar," the Magistrate said to me, just the two of us facing each other over a counter that separated his body from mine.

"And it's not me," I declared, absolutely truthful. I'd sent him a letter requesting a hearing on a petty matter, a fine of $7 plus a penalty of $35 that I felt was unjust. I'd received a summons with no mention of the hearing, and he'd just informed me he'd never received my letter mailed weeks before.

"Sixty-five dollars or five days in jail," he replied, a quick announcement of summary justice in Western Pennsylvania in 1975. "I've listened to so many liars for so many years that I know one when I hear one."

12

For a polygraph test, the tourniquet for conscience clamps one arm while the cummerbund for anxiety circles the chest. A dispassionate examiner sits to test the small tumults of the nervous system, how drama grows from a surplus of lies.

First, he offers irrelevant questions. Eventually, he establishes a cadence for interrogation, tapping out twice-asked queries as control until the rapture of the familiar waylays the practiced lies for circumstance.

The electricity of the body is measured so well the liar must snuff the fuse of falsehood, controlling heart beat and breath with the yoga of evasion, gaining readmittance to the limp life of standing with a drink, early evening, on a lawn, deciding whether to mow the following day, whether the color of sunset means a near future of rain, or the feigned delight for a cloudless day.

13

Once, by malfunction, I was locked in a hands-on museum's antique oscillometric monitor, the cuff refusing to unsnap, and I watched, tugging at its clips, as my systolic number climbed beyond the boiling point for blood, overheating until the room fluttered from such fright I might have been answering questions about the slow, self-murder of envy and the failure to empathize, even lying about my name and address, falsely claiming love for my wife and children, whether I had ever uttered the truth.

14

Still on the Internet, I discover PolygraphNow.com, which lists thousands of lie detector experts. It's a booming service. There's competition for the truth.

The first one I log on to claims to be state of the art. "When the truth matters," it proclaims, expounding on something called the Stoelting CPS II Computerized Polygraph System. The specialties are infidelity, sexual misconduct, and theft. The site promises to "get rid of the suspicion" at the lowest rates. "Call today," it says, so I know that this service costs way more than the $10 per half hour of the LiarCard, so much more that the prices can't be listed for fear of driving customers away.

Instead, the site claims that the other systems I might be considering are no more accurate than chance, which means, if I believe, there are thousands of experts who will provide only the conclusiveness of a coin flip.

15

For a few hours, visiting the nursing home, I manage all the answers I believe my father, at ninety, wants to hear. How I'm happy and successful. How my children thrive. How their children are smart and ambitious.

Bending to let him hug me from his wheelchair, I allow him to hold me as long as he wants. At last, I say, "I love you" directly into the ear with which he can hear, trusting the truth of it to influence his muscles and nerves, letting him hold me until we both control our breathing.

THINGS THAT FALL FROM THE SKY

Rocks

From a freeway overpass in Central Pennsylvania, four teenage boys fling rocks at traffic passing beneath them along Route 80. One misses hitting anything but the highway. One nearly the size of a bowling ball bounces off the cab of a semi. At last, one strikes the windshield of a car heading east. When the car immediately slows, pulls off the highway, and parks, the boys hurry to their car and drive off.

Space Junk

In 1962, a twenty-one pound metal object plummeted from the sky and landed at the intersection of two streets in Manitowoc, Wisconsin. Eventually, it was confirmed to be the remnant of Sputnik IV, becoming the first example of a significant piece of space junk surviving re-entry after falling out of orbit. When first noticed, it was imbedded three inches deep in the asphalt street.

Powder

In 1969, in South Carolina, a white cloud spewed from the new Borden plant near the small town of Chester. It rose and drifted and hovered above the town, eventually beginning to fall. The day became white and sweet like the air above a rolling pin thinning cookie dough. Children stood beside their mothers, their hands clutching toys they would not part with. The weather seemed to cut the neighborhood into the shapes of families. The cloud was soluble on tongues. It surrounded each face. Already there were footprints on sidewalks, the anticipation of brooms. Some of those dusted by that shower took vows. As if time was ending, there were declarations of love and promises to do better. But not for long. The powder turned out to be Borden's nondairy creamer. The company offered reassurance. Though later, when the whitened bathed, some of them stroked the film that had formed along their cheeks, their fingertips dizzy with the wonder of children touching the rouged faces of the dead.

Nuclear Bombs
The United States government calls nuclear bombs that go astray "Broken Arrows." Four such broken arrows fell from the sky on January 17th, 1966 when two US Air Force planes collided over southern Spain. A B-52G bomber was struck by the KC-135 tanker plane sent to perform routine air-to-air refueling and broke apart. Three of the bomber's H-bombs landed in or around Palomares; the fourth landed about five miles offshore in the Mediterranean. There was no nuclear blast, but plutonium was scattered over a wide area.

Rocks
Sharon Budd, a middle school teacher from Ohio, is a passenger in the car the boys hit. She is struck full in the face. In her husband Randy's 911 call, he says, "This is bad. Something came right through the windshield." He is unhurt. So is the driver, his nineteen year-old daughter. "There's a rock that came in," he goes on. "She's grasping for her life. My God, half her brain is gone. Oh, my God." His daughter can be heard screaming during the 911 call.

Space Junk
Nearly every day during the winter when my younger son was thirteen, he searched the sky for the first sign of space junk that was forecast soon to tumble out of orbit. "What if it lands here?" he asked more than once, and each time I told him that was so close to impossible there was no sense even thinking about it. "But not 100% impossible, right?" he said, and he began to research the size and weight of what was about to fall, how much of it might survive re-entry. He relayed the following details to me:

The name of the object is Salyut 7, the last of nine space stations the Soviet Union launched from 1971 to 1982. It blasted off on April 19, 1982, and has stayed aloft for nearly nine years. Six different resident crews have spent time aboard during its operational life. It is about 52 feet long and 13.6 feet across at its widest point. It weighs about 22 tons. A spaceship called Cosmos 1686 is still docked to the station. It weighs just as much as the space station, and all 44 tons of it is about to plummet toward Earth.

Seeds

A father calls his wife and children outside to witness the eastern sky turning dim with clouds the color of blood. They stand transfixed, staring skyward until rain falls like a swarm of sand. They live in Italy. The year is 1897. What falls are seeds, all of them from Judas trees, none of which grow anywhere near them. The light after the shower is so yellow it seems to have traveled from a jaundiced star. The father kneels to run his hands over those seeds, reading the braille of what might be said by a solid rain.

Nuclear Bombs

The bombs that fell near Palomares from the destroyed plane weren't armed, so there was no nuclear explosion. Parachutes attached to the bombs were supposed to bear them gently down to earth, preventing any contamination, but two of the parachutes failed to open, and those bombs blew apart on impact, scattering highly toxic, radioactive plutonium dust, a major hazard to anyone who might inhale it. And there was the issue of finding the one that fell offshore.

Rocks

Randy Budd says his wife had just finished speaking with their eldest son before the vehicle was struck by the rock. After hanging up the phone, his wife asked their son to send her a selfie from his station in Fort Bliss, Texas, which he did. "I really miss you," he texted. Shortly after, the windshield exploded. Randy adds, "I didn't know where her head was."

Space Junk

My son asked to sleep downstairs in the room where his older brother had lived before going off to college. From time to time I caught him walking with his eyes focused on the sky. "Will we be able to see it coming?" he asked, and when I said, "Not likely," he had me go outside with him with binoculars. He worried that most of the late January and early February days were cloudy. By then he understood that the space station and its attached ship would break apart and mostly disintegrate before it reached Earth, but still he worried. "So many pieces makes it worse," he said. The whole thing plunged back to Earth on Feb. 7, 1991, breaking up over Argentina. Some debris was discovered scattered over a town called Capitán Bermúdez. There were no reported injuries.

Small Stones
When I was in first grade I was proud of being able to throw stones across the wide street in front of the house where we rented three upstairs rooms. I stood on the wall that ran up from the sidewalk and waited for cars to drive by in the far lane, tossing small rocks over them as they passed. Standing on the wall gave me the advantage of height. The stones, hardly more than pebbles, looked to my six year-old eyes as if they were arcing down from the sky. Eventually, one fell short and landed on the windshield of a blue car. When the car pulled into the alley beside the house and the driver stepped out, I ran inside, up the stairs and into the room I shared with my older sister. Within a minute a man was speaking with my mother about the small crack the stone had made. The crack, it turned out, was tiny and so far into the corner of the glass that unless it spread, the driver wouldn't ask for money. All I had to do was apologize, forcing the words out between sobs.

Nuclear Bombs
Nobody on the ground in Palomares was killed by the falling bombs. 700 US airmen and scientists were employed to search for bombs and clean up. Three inches of topsoil was removed, sealed in 4,810 barrels and shipped to a storage facility in the United States. Twenty ships, including mine-sweepers and submersibles, were deployed by the US Navy to find the missing bomb that was in the Mediterranean. The cost of the sea search was over $10 million. Four months later, the missing bomb was finally hoisted on board a US warship from a depth of 2,850 ft. How much plutonium is still near Palomares is unknown.

Rocks
The teenage rock throwers' names are brothers Dylan and Brett Lahr, Tyler Porter, and Keefer McGee. McGee was driving his Mitsubishi Eclipse when they stopped on the overpass near Route 80's Milton Exit.

When the car below them slowed, they fled to the house where the brothers lived. They tried to watch a movie, but dying to know how much damage they'd caused, they got in the Lahr's gold Honda Accord and drove past the scene to see what was happening. When they saw a police car, they returned to the house. They went back yet again and saw more police cruisers. The police took notice of the Honda's license plate.

Documents

In 1973 a set of papers fell from a distance higher than a nearby 300-foot radio transmission tower. It looked, to the witness, as if a briefcase had opened, a latch sprung loose among the clouds. A hoax was suspected, but a few lines about the event eventually appeared in a newspaper. The documents, it was reported, were full of graphs and formulas that explained "normalized extinction" and the Davis-Greenstein mechanism of astrophysics.

Nuclear Bombs

My first air raid drill was in second grade. Everyone in the grade school was herded downstairs to the basement and told to stand against a wall away from any windows. Close your eyes, the teacher said, don't open them until I tell you. After that, we had those twice a year. We had fire drills once a month. In third grade we dropped beneath our desks and covered our heads with our hands. "All clear," the teacher said both times. The school was six miles from Pittsburgh. She told us that the city and its steel mills were prime targets. "Pittsburgh is very important," the teacher said, something I always remembered when the nearby fire station tested its air raid siren. "Could we see the bomb falling?" I asked her, and she answered, "Don't you worry about that." Every time I was home alone when the sirens wailed, my father sleeping, my mother at work, I watched the sky believing this was the time the warning was for real.

Rocks

At the hospital, the teacher's forehead and skull cap were removed to allow for swelling in her brain. She had lost an eye and the other was severely damaged. In a short period of time, she underwent five surgeries, first to save her life, then to reconstruct her face, and, at last, to provide her with an artificial skull cap. In the first newspaper report after the boys were arrested, one of them denies throwing any rocks as if abstinence is a synonym for innocence.

Frogs, Toads, Fish

Not rare, these things falling from the sky. In fact, they are so common that a standard reason is provided by scientists — whirlwinds suck up water and carry what's in it until everything falls from the sky.

Nuclear Bombs

A B-52 was flying over North Carolina on January 24, 1961, when it suffered what was reported as a "failure of the right wing." The plane broke apart, and two atom bombs plummeted toward the ground near Goldsboro. The parachute opened on one; it didn't on the other. "The impact of the aircraft breakup initiated the fusing sequence for both bombs," the investigators of the incident reported, an admission that both weapons came very close to detonating. The bomb whose parachute opened landed intact. Fortunately, the pins that provided power from a generator to the weapon had been yanked, preventing it from going off. The bomb with the unopened parachute landed in a free fall. The impact of the crash put it in the "armed" setting, but another part of the bomb needed to initiate an explosion was damaged, and it did not explode. Secretary of Defense Robert McNamara said, "By the slightest margin of chance, literally the failure of two wires to cross, a nuclear explosion was averted."

Rocks

When I search for other incidents of rocks thrown from overpasses onto passing cars and trucks, there are dozens of stories. The one closest to where I live and where Sharon Budd was struck happened shortly after. A man was driving his Kenworth truck on state Route 924 within a few miles of the Budd incident when a rock crashed through his windshield. However, it missed striking him. When I move to recent incidents farther away, I read about a man who was driving home on Interstate 35 near Austin, Texas when a rock came through his windshield and smashed into his face. He is paralyzed on his right side and is unable to talk or write, according to a television report on KEYE. Another station KXAN reports that three other motorists were injured in rock throwing incidents on the same highway within a month of the one that paralyzed that driver.

Concrete

One afternoon, just after recess ended, a corner of concrete from just under the roof of my elementary school broke off and fell fifty feet into the playground. Our teacher kept us in our seats. She told us to pay attention to what we were doing, not what was happening outside, but when school ended, everyone I knew veered out of the path to where the school buses waited to take a look at the crash site. We all knew exactly how long it had been since we had stood in the spot where the stone struck the cement. Last week. Yesterday. That morning. Minutes before.

Space Junk

I look for a more recent example of enormous objects falling from orbit and find the story of the 6.5-ton UARS satellite. NASA's space shuttle Discovery deployed the climate satellite in September 1991. The $750 million satellite was decommissioned by NASA in December 2005. When it fell to Earth, the event was reported this way:

NASA estimates that UARS will come crashing back to Earth Friday night (Sept. 23) or Saturday morning (Sept. 24). At the moment, they're not sure precisely where; pretty much anywhere on the planet between the latitudes of northern Canada and southern South America is a possibility. Researchers further estimate that about 1,170 pounds of UARS' 6.5-ton bulk will survive re-entry. Chances of human casualties are extremely remote; NASA pegs the chance of a piece of UARS debris hitting anybody anywhere in the world at 1 in 3,200.

Nuclear Bombs

According to a Department of Defense document, two months after the close call in Goldsboro, another B-52 was flying in the western United States when the cabin depressurized and the crew ejected, leaving the pilot to steer the bomber away from populated areas. The plane crashed in Yuba City, California, but safety devices prevented the two onboard nuclear weapons from detonating.

Rocks

When asked by reporters who are covering the Sharon Budd story, Pennsylvania state police can't say how many times someone threw an object that struck a vehicle last year, because its database lumps those incidents in with incidents in which something lands on a highway. What is known is that in 2013, troopers responded to 213 "assault-propulsion of missile" incidents that include both categories. The numbers of such incidents was 229 in 2012, and 282 in 2011. What the reporters also learn is that in Pennsylvania, fences are erected on highway overpasses in urban areas that have sidewalks and are near a school or playgrounds. The Gray Hill Road overpass in the New Columbia area from which the rock was thrown that hit the Budd car doesn't meet that criteria because it's in a rural area, with no sidewalk. The overpass is 22 feet high.

Water Balloons

At the beginning of ninth grade, at the high school band picnic, I followed four other freshmen and one sophomore up the winding outside staircase that led to the top of the water tower at Allegheny County's North Park. The sophomore had given us balloons to fill with water and shown us how to tie them securely. I had two that wobbled in my hands. Some of the other boys balanced two in each hand. "There's always somebody who doesn't know we're up here," the sophomore said. He played French horn. I played trombone, and by the time we reached the 100 foot-high observation deck, I was uneasy with the height and being associated with boys who thought tossing water balloons was cool. Every other boy screamed when a balloon burst close enough to somebody to soak them. I was the only one who didn't lean over the railing to see the damage. Before the last balloons were tossed, I made my way down the stairs and hoped that anyone coming up the 154 metal steps would remember that I wasn't part of the group that tossed the balloons, that anyone soaked would see me half way down while the next balloon arced toward them.

Nuclear Bombs

The Defense Department has disclosed 32 accidents involving nuclear weapons between 1950 and 1980. There are at least 21 declassified accounts between 1950 and 1968 of aircraft-related incidents in which nuclear weapons were lost, accidentally dropped, jettisoned for safety reasons or on board planes that crashed. The accidents occurred in various U.S. states, Greenland, Spain, Morocco and England, and over the Pacific and Atlantic oceans and the Mediterranean Sea. Another five accidents occurred when planes were taxiing or parked.

More Powder
On July 10, 1976, an explosion at a northern Italian chemical plant released a thick, white cloud. Close by was the town of Seveso, and the powder quickly settled upon it. Soon small animals began to die. Cats. Dogs. It took four days before people felt sick. They were nauseous. They had blurred vision. And things were worse with their children, who broke out in a skin disease known as chloracne. The town wasn't evacuated until weeks later. The white mist that fell on Seveso was dioxin. After a while, the residents returned. Eventually, babies were born disfigured. Liver disease became common.

Rocks
The police questioned Ron Johnson, who lives only 100 feet from the Gray Hill Road overpass. He mentioned to them that kids had tossed rocks at tractor trailers from the same bridge about seven years ago. "Then they put the signs up, 'No standing on bridge,' and there for a while the cops were coming by on a regular basis checking. But nothing happened, so the cops stopped coming by."

Space Junk
The largest stone meteorite in recorded history struck Earth near Kirin, China in 1976. More than 100 pieces of the original large meteor reached Earth, some of them weighing hundreds of pounds. One weighed 3,902 pounds, the largest ever recovered.

Pennies
When I was fifteen I watched as a friend sailed a penny out a window from the 25th floor of the University of Pittsburgh's Cathedral of Learning. "If you're high enough," he'd said, "a falling penny will kill somebody." We rushed to look down, but I already knew there was no way he could throw it far enough out to have it hit the ground without bouncing off the outside walls that were built wider at the bottom like a narrow wedding cake. When I said so, he threw another. "We should go higher," he said, but we couldn't get access to any of the seventeen floors above us, the full 535 feet of height. Minutes later, on the street, there was no sign of anyone harmed by the pennies he'd tossed from about 300 feet high.

Nuclear Bombs
A website, nuclearsecrecy.com, allows users to simulate nuclear explosions. It says that one bomb the size of the two that fell on North Carolina in 1961 would emit thermal radiation over a 15-mile radius. Wind conditions, of course, could change that. The website warns that calculating casualties is problematic. Population clusters vary. So does topography.

Rocks
There have been reports of fatalities from rock throwing incidents, including two drivers killed by rocks as big as soccer balls tossed onto a German highway in 2000. Like the boys who hit the Budd car, all of those rock throwers were teenagers. They were charged with murder.

Space Junk
Twenty-six large asteroids have exploded in the Earth's atmosphere in the first thirteen years of the 21st Century, all of the explosions registering the power of at least one kiloton. The frequency of an asteroid striking earth with the power to destroy a large city is calculated at about once per century.

Bodies
One famously landed on a car in San Diego, dropping from a mid-air accident like a fantastically narrow storm. The driver and her child were unharmed, but afterward, she had a habit of glancing up like a weather forecaster. An episode of the television series Six Feet Under begins with a scene that recreates this improbable landing.

Rocks
I learn that before the boys threw rocks, they drove through a corn field to see how much damage they could do, and I remember riding through a corn field in a car as a freshman in college. It was October, not July. "We do this every year," the driver, a townie, said. "We're not hurting anything. It'll just all get cut down in a few weeks anyway." I was anxious the entire time we plowed through the stalks, not because I was worried about being caught, but because it was so hard to see that anything could have been in front of us before that driver could react. The farmer, knowing this vandalism happened every October,

could have laid boulders in the field, anticipating the annual car full of teenage jerks.

Space Junk
The largest iron meteorite weighs more than 60 tons. It was discovered in 1920, on a farm in Namibia. It is now a national monument visited by tourists.

More Bodies
It's rare to believe a body is falling from a cloud. It takes height that turns us breathless, a thousand feet or more to make us think "sky." In high school physics class, we learned Newton's Second Law, the one that offers a formula for the acceleration of a falling object: $g=32$ ft. per second squared. The velocity of the falling object could be calculated by the formula $v=g \times time$. The World Trade Centers were over 1300 feet high. The morning of the terrorist attacks distance and speed throttled our breath while suited bodies plunged like drops of a passing shower. Those bodies were falling about 120 miles per hour when they hit the ground. They have been filmed. They have been watched again and again. How some held hands when they leaped. The sky, that morning, was clear.

Nuclear Bombs
In December 1965, a month before the accident at Palomares, the James Bond film Thunderball was released. The story line was eerily similar. Bond's mission was to find atomic bombs that had been lost at sea, and news stories about Palomares made the connection. In real life, it was much harder to first locate, and then recover the bomb from the seabed.

Rocks
Four months after the incident, as part of a plea deal, Keefer McGee agrees to testify against his friends. In court, he says, "We decided to throw rocks at cars, just go out and be bad." He describes how, when they reached the overpass, Dylan and Tyler jumped out armed with rocks they'd gathered earlier. "There was a loud crash when Dylan's stone hit," he says. "We all laughed as we drove away."

More Bodies

The newly completed World Trade Center is 1776 feet tall with its antenna, a 408-foot spire, included. The builders have called the antenna a mast to insure the Trade Center is judged the tallest building in the United States rather than the Willis (formerly Sears) Tower in Chicago. The new Trade Center has fewer floors but has been designated tallest by the Council on Tall Buildings and Urban Habitat. In Chicago, years ago, my friend refused to go up in the Sears Tower, so I went alone. As always when I was close enough to the edge to see down into the city, every instinct told me to stay back, but the safety shield was high enough for even me to relax. Even so, riding down in the elevator felt like rescue.

Nuclear Bombs
University of California-Los Angeles researchers estimate that, respectively, Hiroshima and Nagasaki had populations of about 330,000 and 250,000 when they were bombed in August 1945. By that December, the cities' death tolls included, by conservative estimates, at least 90,000 and 60,000 people. All of the United States nuclear bombs involved in major accidents since then were far more powerful than those.

Rocks
Sharon Budd spent weeks in an induced coma. It took thirteen hours of surgery to reconstruct her face. The surgeon said it was the worst case he'd ever seen. In a later interview, Randy Budd talked about growing up in a rough Ohio neighborhood, learning early to take care of himself. How that affected his feelings about the four boys. "There's some of that in me," he said. "That's one way I have of how, if someone does something wrong to you, to handle it."

More Bodies
People have experimented with postures in the air to acquire maximum velocity. The record free fall speed is 330 mph within ordinary atmosphere. However, claims have been made for falling at beyond the speed of sound from the upper atmosphere. Jumping from the stratosphere in 2012, Felix Baumgartner became the first man to break the speed of sound in freefall. He climbed to 128,100 feet in a helium-filled balloon.

Recently, Alan Eustace, a senior vice president at Google, fell from the top of the stratosphere, plummeting nearly 26 vertical miles in the span of about 15 minutes. In doing so, he broke Baumgartner's 2012 record for world's highest-altitude freefall. The official figure on Eustace's maximum altitude was given as 135,890 feet, or 25.74 miles. Baumgartner held on to the overall speed record, however. On his return to Earth, Eustace achieved a top speed of 822 miles per hour, breaking the sound barrier and generating a sonic boom, but shy of Baumgartner's Guinness Book of Records approved speed of 833.9 mph.

Rocks
In October, when Sharon Budd steps out of the Geisinger Medical Center for the first time, she wears a pink #BuddStrong t-shirt. Her artificial skull is covered by a pink and white knit cap. Outside the rehab facility, she is filmed ringing a victory bell reserved for patients who overcome long odds. When she first entered the facility, she was so confused she couldn't manage any of the therapy. Three months since the incident, she has no memory of it. I watch the video of the event several times. As she walks, Sharon Budd is braced on both sides by smiling attendants. At the victory bell ceremony, she is still lightly supported. According to her doctor, she is now "nearly independent, walking with a little assistance, able to take care of herself."

Rocks
In November, Sharon Budd's family notices seepage coming from a scar that runs across her forehead. She has to undergo a sixth surgery at Geisinger Medical Center to treat an infection underneath her artificial skull. The cap is removed and has to remain off for four to six weeks. Now she must wear a protective helmet but is able to return home. However, she will need to come back to Geisinger every two weeks for an exam.

Rocks
The two boys who were seventeen at the time want to be tried as juveniles. The lawyers for all the boys want certain evidence to be suppressed when their clients come to trial. Most important, they say, is not to admit as evidence the 911 call made by Mr. Budd. Likewise, pictures of Mrs. Budd should not be permitted to be shown. They are prejudicial, the lawyers claim. These exhibits are too emotionally charged.

YAMS

A few years ago, at my wife's urging, we began to eat sweet potatoes in place of the familiar white ones of a lifetime's eating. Or they might be yams. When I look up the difference, I discover that there are varieties of sweet potatoes, from yellow and mealy to orange and smooth, and none of them is a yam, a tropical root whose name has been stolen for marketing reasons.

What I know about yams without reading an article is they're orange inside and that half the time we put them back in the oven for another fifteen minutes because they're rock-like, even after an hour of baking, when we test them for eating. When I read an article, I add a few details: Sweet potatoes are the ones that taper at both ends to a point; yams have more sugar than sweet potatoes; despite their similarities, yams and sweet potatoes aren't even related.

What else? I refused them when I was a boy. I believed real potatoes were white, and they could be counted on to taste good no matter how they were made—mashed with gravy, fried with onions, baked with butter, scalloped with an extra dose of cheese, and best of all—French fried with enough salt to pucker my lips.

Yams were what my sister and my parents ate at Thanksgiving, misshapen and orange on their plates beside white meat and three kinds of vegetables. My plate was all mashed potatoes and gravy, white and dark meat both covered with gravy, stuffing sopped with more gravy, and a spoonful of peas just large enough to keep my father from dumping twice as many on my plate to make sure I wasn't stunting my growth.

Yams sat in bins at the grocery store. They didn't come, like white potatoes, in the five and ten pound bags my mother lugged home. Yams were in stories about Africa. Tribes ate them, villagers who still carried spears and stared at missionaries who visited them to explain Jesus. I was out of college before I willingly ate a yam, filling a groove I cut in its skin with butter and brown sugar a few minutes before I took it from the oven.

A few years later, when I had children of my own who complained about yams, wishing for French fries or mashed potatoes with gravy, the milk carton that sat on the table during dinner always featured the face of a missing child. "Have You Seen Me?" its caption read, and those faces reminded me to be thankful even as my children yammered their petty complaints. As the three of them poked at their half-eaten yams, wasting what was left after a half hour of whining, those milk carton faces kept my anger in check.

Eventually, milk cartons stopped showing lost children and sweet potatoes became the norm at dinner, but now those missing children's faces show up inside my income tax instructional booklet. I turn the pages, looking at each child, and every one seems hopelessly lost. How are they chosen from among the thousands who are painfully eligible?

There are computer projections now of how those children, some of them lost for five or even ten years, would look in the present. My eyes shift from the photograph to the computer image and back again, searching for how facial features have been transformed. After a few minutes, I try not to imagine what most missing children end up looking like.

Now I have a grandson who refuses yams. He's seven years old. In about ten years he'll be won over, I think, but I don't tell him that, and I don't mention a word about the story I happened upon this week about how three pupils in a Nigerian elementary school told their headmistress that another boy had been transformed into a yam after accepting candy from a stranger. The headmistress followed the boys to the yam and carried it to the police, who kept it, drawing hundreds of people to come to the station to see.

The police organized a search for the stranger. Seven years have passed since then, and no one has been found.

Neither has a boy who has just disappeared in a nearby town. Crowds of people are searching. Something related to the investigation has been found in a wooded area, but the police, for now, aren't revealing what it is. No one is suggesting that the object is the boy transformed.

DRAGGING THE FOREST

You Know

The woman whose one daughter was buried by her killer says she wants to talk to someone who will write everything down. She means "to say her piece" in the paper where my column is printed twice a month, but she lapses into silence after she begins, "It's awful to bear."

I nod like I know what it is to have a child found after eight months in the ground. The four rooms she rents face a wall that keeps the Susquehanna River from flooding her street and the next seven blocks before the city slopes up to hillsides where the rich build. "Over there," she finally says, "you know," meaning beyond that wall where her daughter has surfaced because the shallow grave eroded during the spring flood.

She displays a small set of photographs I shuffle through with my eyes, embarrassed to lay my hands on them. On the left is her daughter at twenty, taken, she says, "Just the month before." Across the street from her rented rooms, the miles-long length of the flood wall has been painted with the words "Thank You Wall," the phrase repeated dozens of times in the same script after April's flood crested six inches from its brink.

"Beforehand is when you know what's already happened," she says. "It doesn't take Thomas to touch the grave," trusting a Bible reference for emphasis. "Study her now," she says. "Find the words." Those photographs, one after the other going back to childhood, begin to speak.

The First Dark Glasses
The nearest highway lights, a half mile away, are aspirin. While we walk the shoulder, a friend talks about the queen who bearded herself before ceremonies, convincing her soldiers to obey. When trucks rush by, the air between us rattles; when the road clears, the night is footsteps.

The first dark glasses, I tell him, were worn by judges to hide how they felt about evidence and the prisoners before them. "Everybody needs dark glasses," he says. "There's no end of horrible people." When, even after three trucks have passed and the road clears, lights seem to be coming from both sides like testimony.

Stories
My daughter says that three men, this year, have jerked themselves off while she walked near them in New York. She names old high school teachers who suggested sex, the way they managed ambiguity to protect themselves from guilt or shame.

We're talking this way because a man, this afternoon, showed my daughter his back yard and asked her what she imagined fish did in winter, guiding her toward his shadowed pond, asking, at last, how long I'd be gone from the house we were visiting. And because he's not a memory, because he's standing on his screened-in porch fifty feet from us, we lower our voices when we start to talk about the needs we keep to ourselves until some of us eagerly surrender.

Local Girls
A young girl's murder is the lead story in the local newspaper for three days. On the television news, it remains a feature for nearly a week. Only a few hours after her disappearance a search party had been formed; within an hour her body was found in the woods near her home. The father is interviewed. A grandmother stands awkwardly in front of a camera. The girl is seven years-old; it's a wonder they can be

coherent. Neighbors express astonishment a girl can be snatched and murdered right from the block on which she lives. The police shake their heads and look grave.

The girl had been missing such a short time there was some hope when the search began. Not like the girl, slightly older, who disappeared a few years ago in another town within thirty miles of where I live. By the time she was found, the discovery, deep in a wooded area, was called "skeletal remains." That time she was snatched right from her house during the night.

Rumors begin in the community and reach our town, twenty miles away, by the day after the murder. Most of them are full of serial pedophile killers, references back to unsolved cases within a hundred miles. The most convincing story features a teenage boy seen playing with the girl a short time before she didn't return when called. The police are close-mouthed about the ongoing investigation.

More Stories

My wife begins with hiding in a ditch as a child, pressing herself to the dirt as if her seventh grade homeroom teacher was evaluating her bomb drill form.

The men in the truck parked twenty feet from her joked about the fresh meat that had turned their truck around. One of them said, "She'll have a story to tell tomorrow if we find her" while he pissed upon the shoulder, so close she heard the hiss of contact just before a quirk of heavy traffic chased their lust away.

"I lay there and waited a long time after they drove away," she says. "I could see both my house and my friend's house from where I stood when I finally got up. I never told my mother. If I'd told my father, he would have punished me for walking home in the dark alone."

"Maybe they were playing with you," I say, and she makes a face that screams "Asshole!"

Chat Rooms

Where I live the towns are small and scattered, so even a few recent cases seem like an epidemic. Among the others I discover is a case where the child met her killer on line. For a while that crime created publicity about the danger of unsupervised use of computers and who might be lurking in chat rooms, trolling for victims. Men in rooms designated for teens or younger who disguise themselves with nicknames and schoolyard slang. The stuff of movies with R ratings attached.

This time, to see for myself, I try a search, beginning with rape and murder and children. Hundreds of sites scroll down, most of them appearing to be anecdotal or analytical. And then I notice a number of what look like violent porn sites: "Scream and Cream." "Hanging Whores." I follow the trail of sadistic key words to snuff. Dozens of sites are listed, many of them speaking to the mild narcotic habits described in centuries-old novels. Others take me to speculations on the availability of "real" snuff films. Finally, one takes me to The Snuff Top 100. I click on a site that promises "photo galleries." It delivers.

In one section I find twenty-eight pages of thumbnail photographs of apparently murdered women. There are thirty pictures per page. Most of the 840 women are naked. When I click on a picture to enlarge it, a message tells me the privilege to do so requires a monthly fee.

I go back to the main page and click on "chat." A minute later I'm in a room featuring conversation about necrophilia. Underneath the space for messages are instructions on how to move to other such rooms or create ones of my own.

Choose a name, the directions say, the word guest already present in the space provided. I call myself guest12345. "Name taken," the screen says. "Choose another within 60 seconds." I add a 6, and the chat room accepts me.

I try "murder" and "snuff," but there's no one. I try "rape," and there is just one name listed: "comingforyou." Whoever it is, doesn't respond.

I try "snuffsex," and a window opens that shows 14 names equally divided between male and female sounding. Nobody sends me a message, so I type in a nickname of my own: Strangler. "Name taken" appears. "Choose another within 60 seconds." Strangler2, I type, and that works. Nobody contacts me, so I send private messages to four female names.

The only one who answers claims she lives in Michigan and wants me to kill her and her daughter, the daughter first while she watches. I figure her for a man concocting a fantasy.

I leave and return, minutes later, with a female name. This time I get five private messages in less than a minute. Beheadher. NomoreO24U. Neckbreaker. MrPerv. Blackdemon. Three of them seem to be creating fantasies about me as Schoolgirl. They ask what I look like. What I'm wearing.

One claims he wants to kill a girl for real and asks if I'm interested. To keep him going, I say Yes.

Where do you live? he types. Where can we meet?

Trolling

I go to the mall for lunch. During the time I eat two slices of pizza, seven girls who look to be between the ages of ten and fourteen pass by me. Six of them go by in pairs, but the seventh, about twelve years old, is apparently by herself. Every one of them looks careless. After they pass, I watch to see if anyone follows them.

Two minutes later, leaving the mall, I see the girl who is alone. She has bought a soft pretzel and takes bites as she walks. I stay behind her past two stores, cursing her parents. I swing right, going out to my car before I begin to imagine tomorrow's news.

The Murder Interview

After the boy who killed his daughter is arrested, the local girl's father speaks to a newspaper reporter. "She was riding on his shoulders," he says. "She waved at me."

It's his description of the last time he saw his daughter alive. She is, we all know now, just minutes from death. The father returned to his yard work. The girl, according to another witness, climbed down and held that boy's hand like a small sister, beginning a walk in the woods. After

98

that, it's speculation.

The boy is fifteen. The girl's body is found undressed, beaten and strangled. The father, later in the article, remembers that boy helping with the search, calling her by a nickname. He remembers the way she bounced on that boy's shoulders, laughing. Like on a carousel, he says, like she was at the school picnic out to the park, the bumper cars and the tilt-a-whirl coming next. He lights a cigarette, and I remember the weight of my children through my shoulders.

The Worst Thing
Several years ago, a child in our small town survived a rape and attempted murder. She was tied to a tree in a wooded area and molested, but the rapist, according to the part of his confession published in the newspaper, lost his nerve about killing her. "I wanted to do something so terrible I'd be executed," he explained to the police.

He was thinking correctly about nearly everyone's reaction to child rape and murder. When I read his story, I thought of the old film M in which Peter Lorre starred as a child murderer. After he's imprisoned, the other inmates judge him as the worst possible human being, relegating him to the lowest circle in their Dantesque criminal hell. I know I didn't disagree.

The fifteen-year-old boy who killed the seven-year-old girl appears on the evening news. He's being transported to prison, and for a minute the cameras follow him taking the slow walk to a patrol car. He looks naïve. He looks ordinary. He looks like somebody who would offer to shovel my driveway for $10 to help him pay for a new stereo. BURN IN HELL, a sign raised from the crowd says. EXECUTE HIM says another. A woman spits at him. The police have a struggle keeping the small crowd under control. If the police drove away without the boy, it seems likely he would be lynched.

Dragging the Forest
My father, once, explained to me how he was asked to participate in a search party. He was a Boy Scout. Incredibly, someone thought it was a good idea to have his troop members help search for a missing boy.

"Up there," he said, nodding to our left. We were driving past the area near Pittsburgh where the search had taken place. The woods were still there because of the steep slope that pitched down to where we were driving along the Allegheny River. "They told us to spread our arms and walk in a line. There were men among us who kept reminding us to keep our fingers touching. We hiked up that hill, moved sideways, then hiked back down. We sidestepped again and started back up, and then that boy was found."

My father had waited until I was fifty years old to tell me that story. I didn't say anything when he finished. "It was just about this time of year," he finally said. "A day just like today. The boy, of course, was dead. He was tied to a tree. His bag of newspapers was still there. He was a paper boy."

From where we were driving, in the early evening, the river looked black. "I heard one of the boys from another troop scream," my father said. "And then a second boy screamed." Who would ask, I thought, young boys to conduct such a search? Football scores came on the radio. The teams my father was interested in were Pitt, Army, Navy, and Notre Dame. When the announcer finished, my father looked at me. "You think there's a way of knowing ahead of time?" he said. "You think you could save someone?"

INEXPLICABLE

1

The newspaper's lead story is a murder in the small college town where I live. Something rare, the first, according to the story, in twenty-four years. An elderly woman has been beaten to death, her husband found unresponsive in a nearby chair. He is a retired teacher, a recent stroke victim. Nothing is missing from the house. No motive is apparent. "Inexplicable," the police say, but add that they have a person of interest.

2

At my recent fiftieth class reunion, my best high school friend and I remembered "the punch" in detail. During a junior high basketball drill, my friend completed his turn and, while jogging to his place in line, paused to slam his fist into my stomach. Not a word was exchanged. I doubled up. I missed one rotation and then got back in line. My friend had already moved on to take another pass to begin a three-man weave. No one else seemed to notice. More than fifty years later, although we remembered the practice shirts we wore, the nature of the drill, the dimensions of the gym, and even how the walls underneath the baskets were padded because they were so close to the baseline, neither of us could remember the reason for the punch. "Inexplicable," my friend said, and with fifty years of catching up to do, we moved to other topics.

3

Several months ago, the escalator of a crowded airport steepened by my luggage and fatigue and a nudge in the back from a teenager's duffel bag, I remembered a colleague telling me that a student has sued her college because it failed to account for her allergies to escalators, tall people, and cactus. He wanted me to laugh, perhaps be thankful that student didn't attend the university where we teach.

"The fuck, right?" he added, and I heartily agreed until, two weeks later, a student of mine I'll call Bradley, in an email addressed, he said, solely to me, claimed I towered over him when we sat in my office because the chair I offered was set lower than mine. A paragraph later he mentioned that when followed down the stairs by his classmates in the refurbished house where our workshop classes are taught, he was terrified he'd be shoved from behind because they, just like I did, "have it in for me."

After reading the note I turned and looked at the small cactus I keep on a bookshelf near the ordinary, school-issued chair he had referenced. Even if that student thrust an arm out to the side, it seemed a safe distance away from being touched.

4

The day after the murder is publicized, the names of the victim and her husband are released in the newspaper. I recognize the retired teacher's name. One, maybe two, of my three children took driver's education from him twenty-five years ago. A former mayor praises the victim for her decades of work in the borough office. Kind, he says. Greeted every visitor with a smile. So devoted to her job as secretary she never once complained about having to attend all those public meetings that dragged on forever.

Altogether, there are two columns embellished with human interest anecdotes, pictures of two interviewed neighbors off to the side. Both of them say the same thing. Such a shock. A devoted couple. "The sweetest little man" is how one of them describes the husband. She says she was once his driver's ed. student. "So gentle." She's forty, my daughter's age, but I don't remember her being in our house. She's shown standing with her children in her yard, which has the same well-kept look as the yard surrounding the house where the killing took place.

That house immediately looks familiar because it is two blocks from where my family once lived for five years.

When I call my wife, who is in California for a few weeks visiting our daughter, the first thing she says when I give her the news about the murder is "I always thought he was a nice guy. Gentle."

5

Later that night at the fifty-year class reunion I ran into Rick Selby, an old classmate. I shook his hand, smiled, and let him tell me a few things about his job and where he lived. I didn't ask him why, over fifty years ago, he had punched a girl in the ground floor hallway of our high school, becoming the only guy I had ever seen slug a girl. I moved on to another handshake, but I kept my eye on Rick Selby for a few more minutes, remembering.

We'd been standing in the hall after lunch, a couple of minutes to kill before Mr. Brody's plane geometry class. Probably talking about girls or basketball or a difficult, assigned proof, things we did with two spare minutes in tenth grade, and what I could still see clearly at that reunion was how perfect Holly Miller, a junior, looked as she walked towards us. "Hi," I managed to say.

She smiled. "Hi, there," she answered, maybe not even remembering just who I was.

Rick Selby called her by her last name. It sounded so odd, she stopped. "Rick?" she said, as if she were trying to place him.

By then Rick Selby was all clenched teeth and reddening face. He stepped forward and rammed his fist into her stomach, a solar plexus shot. "Oh," she breathed, all exhale followed by the silence you hear when somebody lands flat on his back. Rick Selby ran, leaving me to explain to Holly why I was the kind of person who'd hang out in the halls with a psychopath.

Nobody else had seen it happen. I didn't, five minutes later, think I'd seen it happen either. But at the reunion, when I settled in to talk with my best friend, he said, "You and Selby have a good talk about his girl-punch?"

6

"College counselors have their hands full," my colleague said when word had gotten around about my chairs and stairs case because my student had voiced his complaint about my "bullying" a few times in the dorm where he lived. When I suggested to the counseling center that Bradley bore speaking to, they indicated, without providing details, that he already kept a weekly appointment.

I answered my colleague by nodding toward the coffee mug sitting on one of the bookcases in my office. "You can't make this stuff up," was spelled out on its surface, an advertisement for the joys of writing creative nonfiction.

"I should write more nonfiction," he said.

"Maybe Bradley will sign up for independent writing," I said.

"Maybe you can entertain him every week until he decides what scares him about you."

I was giving it my best bravado, but a few days later, arms loaded with books, I reevaluated those stairs, this time recalling Andy Graber, who shoved a third-grade boy down the thirteen wooden steps of our elementary school, the ones that ended in cement painted the silver and blue of our school colors, the surface slick across our mascot's sled-dog face. Cradling seven volumes, I felt dressed like a victim, recollecting how spelling, geography, and arithmetic flew from the hands of Pete Craig before he followed those textbooks down the steps to the miracle of cuts and bruises but nothing broken while my second grade teacher shouted, "You crazy boy, you!" as she rushed past Andy Graber and down those stairs.

7

The person of interest turns out to be the retired, stroke-stricken teacher. The police say they have no other suspects. This was not a home invasion, the police chief says. The wife died, he goes on, from multiple trauma inflicted by a weapon found at the scene. The police are waiting to speak with the husband, but after several days, he remains unresponsive and in critical condition. No comment is made about how curious it is that a stroke victim could beat his wife to death.

There's no sign of a neighbor or old student talking nice in this article. And there's no sign of the driver's ed. teacher's old friend and his response to accidentally discovering the slaughter when he'd stopped by to check up, something he did so frequently that the victim had given him a key to the house. Nobody, not yet, had interviewed him about his own introduction to the inexplicable, happening upon his unresponsive friend and his dead wife.

The report reprints paragraphs from previous articles, including the lines about the last murder in the borough, in order to emphasize how the town has always been a neighborhood where violence is as rare as a tornado or a Democrat elected to political office.

My wife, from California, reminds me that the murder from twenty-four years ago was a two-year-old child thrown against an apartment wall by his father. "He never gave a reason except he 'lost it,'" she says.

As she speaks, I remember that the child-killer had lived three blocks from the new house we had recently moved into.

8

A high school incident I talked to no one about at the reunion began when another basketball friend Rich Hastings asked me to follow him into the boy's room as soon as we finished eating lunch. Rich didn't explain why, but we were friends and it seemed important. Waiting for him was Fred Karras, who was the only 10th grader I knew who lifted weights. He looked older than us, for sure, all chest and shoulders and the hint of a forbidden mustache. He had a boy with him I didn't recognize, and Fred handed his shirt to him while Rich took his off and handed it to me. They were in t-shirts now, and Fred snap-locked the bathroom door. Nobody said a word until they laid into each other, swinging hard, thumping each other. It was unlike any fight I'd seen or would see in high school. No pushing and shoving, just punches to the face and body until Rich lost his balance and fell, his head thunking against one of the sinks.

Rich sat still for a few seconds while I heard pounding on the door.

"Open up," I heard, and recognized the voice of our geometry teacher Mr. Brody, a former wrestling coach who had a reputation for a short temper. Fred helped Rich stand. They washed their faces without a word and put their shirts on. Just then the door opened, a janitor standing beside Mr. Brody, a crowd of students behind them.

We walked out without speaking, Mr. Brody eyeing us. He knew Rich and me as "good kids." We kept walking and never heard a word about it from anyone else. Fred wasn't at the reunion, but in the program he'd let everyone know he had been a private detective. Rich, who moved to California a few months later, never said a word about motive. I didn't ask, and I never said a word about the fight to anyone, a sequence so inexplicable it feels like I'm making it up as I write.

9

Pete Craig, who returned to school two days after being shoved down the stairs, was my new neighbor. My family had moved in December, and there, in January, attending second grade in a new school, I was happy to have someone I'd played board games with over Christmas vacation to sit beside on the school bus. Even better, because Pete was in third grade, he added a bit of protection for "the new boy" on a bus that carried grades one through six.

For nearly two weeks after school took up again, Pete, sitting two or three rows behind Andy Graber, a skinny blond third grade boy, chanted "Andy Gump from the City Dump" every time the bus approached Andy's stop. By the second week I'd chimed in. Where Andy lived was a mess. The yard was littered with a couple of junked cars and an assortment of old appliances. The house itself was shabby and set below the level of the road so Andy had to descend a short flight of wooden stairs after he got off the bus two stops before ours. Pete never sat directly behind Andy. The two or three rows meant Pete raised his voice, that half the bus could hear, and even though I was younger and smaller, Pete had been singing his song of ridicule long before I rode that bus and sat beside him, so Andy had reason to single him out.

Not inexplicable at all, Andy's vengeance. But for the rest of the school year, though he stopped shouting his rhyme, Pete still chanted at Andy when he passed his seat getting on the bus after school. I wondered whether Andy's father owned guns. I moved away from Pete in the bus.

10

The counseling center kept me informed about my student accuser. Each report said Bradley was making "promising progress." However, Bradley took to wearing a hoodie to class. My colleague, from time to time, asked how Ted Kuchinski was doing.

Before the semester ended, Bradley broke down in class, bolting off to the bathroom just across the hall where everyone in the class could hear him berate himself and slam the walls with his fists. "You fucking pussy," he said over and over, and I tried to tell myself he was admonishing himself for not standing up for his ideas in class rather than for not shooting me and whichever students he held a grudge against.

My colleague, who had a workshop of his own in the adjoining room, hurried to the bathroom door, which was unlocked. He led the boy into a small mailroom where we tried to talk him down at least far enough to walk him to the counseling center next door. "We continue to believe he is not a danger to others" is the report I received the following day. The semester was nearly over. He continued to complain in his workshop critique letters. He sent me another email rant.

I told the counseling center that the first time Bradley complained by email I answered him by email and suggested we talk, but he didn't show up. The second time, I asked him to stay after class, but he walked right out. The third time I took advantage of the word getting around to come to the counseling center in person because I found myself watching his hands when he entered the room. I paid attention when he reached into the backpack he always carried until he extricated a book or a notebook. Even worse, he was always the first person in the room every Tuesday and Thursday, and he always chose the chair beside me directly to my left so I had trouble keeping him in sight. I'd be dead in a heartbeat if he wanted it that way.

And no, I said, I'd never seen anyone picking on Bradley, but for weeks now, he'd also written messages on all of his workshop critique letters, claiming persecution and humiliation, saying how much he hated everyone, including me, for allowing it.

11
One week after the murder, the police release additional details. The woman's body was found on the living room floor covered by a blanket, the teacher sitting in a nearby chair spattered with blood, the weapon a bloody hammer lying on a counter. Several empty vials of prescription drugs were also found at the scene. The police chief reiterates that the frail, retired stroke victim is the only suspect. There is no change in his condition.

12
I was once a high school teacher. To replace me when I resigned, the school hired a woman who had substituted for years. Within a few weeks, a tenth-grade boy used his fist on that woman. "I hope you have a baby in there," he screamed, smacking the pillow of her stomach.

She wasn't pregnant, but when I heard that story from a former colleague, I fantasized about other teachers exacting revenge, beating that boy, but what happened was she resigned on the spot, the boy was suspended for ten days, the maximum, and a man was hired to take that woman's place.

No one ever explained the boy's motive. The boy refused to talk.

13
The year before Bradley accused me of insensitivity and bullying, I'd had a brief back-and-forth with the counseling center. That time the center contacted me first, and the young man in question, it turned out, always sat directly to my right on Monday, Wednesday, and Friday. However, Chad was always friendly. He stayed after class to "just talk." He took pictures of me with his phone, surprising me as I gathered books and manuscripts. He posted a few on Facebook, and they seemed harmless, and when some other students "liked" those pictures, it felt fan-club-like, something I felt good about until my wife said, "You

shouldn't encourage that."

The counseling center asked for privacy; they brought up confidentiality and then let me know that young man had serious anger issues. "I don't see them," I said, and there was a pause before they explained that Chad was likely to be expelled for being a threat to others.

Chad had drawn stabbing pictures on his blue-lined notebook paper, crude drawings of bodies lying in pools of blood. Whether by design or through carelessness, the center didn't know for certain, Chad had left those pictures in a public space in his dorm room. Before I could say "fantasy," a representative from the student life office told me Chad had labeled the victims with the names of students who lived in his hall, that both victims were resident assistants, that Chad had more than minor issues with authority. I decided to do what I could to defend him. I wrote a letter expressing my sense that Chad wasn't a threat. Regardless, he was expelled.

14

My father disapproved of many things I said or did, but he hit me only once. I was in sixth grade, eleven years old. Amy Burchfield, the heaviest girl in my class, had declared in a voice everybody on the school bus could hear, that the only reason I'd won a prize for being "the outstanding sixth grade boy" was because I was always brown-nosing.

"You should see her," I said at the dinner table that night. "She's such a fat pig."

My father slapped me across the face. He didn't speak, and neither did my sister or my mother. I finished dinner and, as always, cleared my dishes.

My mother, later that evening, sat down beside me on the couch as I watched television. "Watch your mouth around your father," she said, and then stood up and walked away, leaving me with an episode of Dobie Gillis.

15

As the murder story lingers on without any sort of resolution, the newspaper limits its coverage, most of it boilerplate that references "stroke victim" and "unresponsive." I find myself wondering how someone might feel about being comforted and reassured every day by his good-intentioned wife. Whether it's not inexplicable at all to react with anger at what somebody might feel is a "hospice voice." That kindness confirms dependency. Or worse.

16

A few months after he was expelled, Chad asked to be my Facebook friend. Several years later, graduated from another college, he continues to post. One of the photos he took of me is still available, a stuffed duck his then-current girlfriend brought to class every day somehow moved close to the books I'd brought to class.

One day he sends me a note about a half-century-old *Life* magazine article on play therapy. The article reports on a psychiatrist treating a boy, aged ten, who heaves clay against the life-sized scrawled drawing of his brother, the body chalked on the wall like the dead. The patient declares he is happy now, and though not exactly in love with that hated brother, he's stopped screaming, "I want to kill you!" like Andy Graber did, standing so still at the top of the emptied staircase, he could have been scribbled on the air.

Or, though Chad doesn't say it, like he had suggested with his drawings years before.

17

Recently, when I visited a hospital as preparation for minor surgery, I listed my allergies for the attending nurse and explained how, thirty years before, I'd grown into asthma. At the time, I'd been tested for allergies, coming up positive for dust, pine trees, cats, hamsters, sulfites, heavy cream, and several more, one environmental hazard after another finally overcoming my immune system. She entered the items into the computer without expression, my allergies or the extent of them becoming nothing extraordinary. What medicines do you take? She asked next, and she recorded the medical name for the contents of my inhaler and the generic name for the Singulair I swallow each morning.

For a moment I thought of that woman who sued her college about escalators and tall people and cactus, how she'd included an allergy to the color mauve as well. Instead, I mentioned my anxiety with allergies and their medicines ever since a foot doctor who lived nearby had died from a bee sting despite using his prescribed antidote.

And once I got started, making myself anxious enough to spike my blood pressure reading, I told her how my daughter, for her twenty-first birthday, swallowed a liqueur speckled with gold dust that a friend bought for her, and her throat shut tight as if it wanted nothing more. After she gasped and wheezed, after her friends begged the bar for doctors, she saw strangers stand and ask what and how like children watching a magician. "I could have died a metaphor," she'd told me, "the woman with an allergy to gold."

18

I look up play therapy online and discover that it is still used. There are paragraphs explaining that the child is informed that he or she can say or play or do anything desired while in the office as long as no one gets hurt, and that what is said and done in the office will be kept private unless the child is in danger of harming himself. As the child plays, the therapist begins to recognize themes and patterns or ways of using the materials that are important to the child, the play reflecting issues that are important to the child and typically relevant to their difficulties.

Near the end of the article I read, it says, "When the child's symptoms have subsided for a stable period of time and when functioning is adequate with peers and adults at home, in school, and in extracurricular activities, the focus of treatment will shift away from problems and onto the process of saying goodbye."

19

After nearly two months, the murder case has disappeared from the newspaper for fifteen days, the phrase "unresponsive" became unnecessary to repeat. However, there is a rumor that the driver's ed. teacher shows signs of coming out of his coma. "Then we'll know everything," a neighbor said yesterday with the confidence of a small child.

This morning I walk from my house to the one my family lived in thirty years ago. Its number is 401; the house where the murder occurred is 616. I can see it from the yard I used to mow. It takes me fewer than

500 steps to arrive at the site. Someone has tended the yard, the grass mown in late May.

I loop up past the high school and the intermediate school and enter what, twenty-four years ago, was the most well-kept low-income housing complex I've ever seen. Both of my sons delivered newspapers here, but now it belongs to the university for which I work, the apartments upscale housing for juniors and seniors. I remember which building, but not in which apartment the toddler was killed. Without difficulty, I can see my current house from here. The walk home takes fewer than 900 steps.

20
At the 50th reunion, Amy Burchfield said, "Hello, Gary," and hugged me. For a few minutes, we told each other quick summaries of our lives. "You've done well," she said. She was still heavy, but there were at least a dozen heavier women at the reunion.

21
None of the newspaper reports ever include an interview with the man who was the first to happen upon the murder scene. Whether he touched the victim or the killer first. Whether he touched either of them. Whether he touched anything at all, calling 911 from just inside the door.

And regardless of his actions, what he was thinking, right then, when he walked in on something inexplicable.

22
When I read further about play therapy I come across the following statement: "Aftercare children sometimes return to therapy for additional sessions when they experience a setback that cannot be easily resolved."

Though I never had him in class again, before Bradley graduated I moved my small cactus to a windowsill, telling myself more light would make it thrive. Within weeks it shriveled. A secretary who examined it proclaimed I'd overwatered, killing that cactus because I equated full sunlight with insatiable thirst.

PROXIMITY

When my wife and I arrive in Los Angeles, my daughter says a peacock's blown into her neighborhood from Griffith Park, driven by the record Pacific wind of two days before. "Lucky for that bird," Shannon tells us, "we have all these trees and roofs."

When I ask where it is, she says, "You'll see it. It was still here this morning."

Happy to relax on her balcony after the long flight, I scan every possible roosting place, but the pine trees and the apartment house roofs below yield nothing. The traffic on Los Feliz Boulevard is as incessant as ever. I follow the setting sun around back, and when I slouch in a soft chair on her small patio that is at least sheltered from the traffic noise, a peacock seems more likely to show up.

Sure enough, though I see nothing on the steep, wooded hill that sweeps up behind my daughter's rental house, I hear squawking, so I walk inside to tell her I heard the bird. "That's not the peacock," Shannon says. "That's the woman who lives in one of the apartments below us."

When we hear the squawking again, Shannon explains that by last night (only a day after the peacock's arrival), her neighbor had learned to mimic the peacock's odd call. "She has it almost perfect," my daughter says. "She even squawks over the sound of traffic. You'll see her while you're here. She's sure to come up the stairs from her apartment to visit."

I hear another call, but I keep to myself that it arrives like a sound check for lunacy.

*

As always, when we visit for a week or more, my wife and I rent an apartment on the other side of Los Feliz Boulevard, a short walk away from the cramped space Shannon shares with her two young daughters. In the morning, I use the fitness room; nearly every afternoon I walk to the movies or the library. My wife swims in the apartment's outdoor pool every afternoon.

On the second day of this trip, she tells me helicopters hovered overhead while I sat through *End of Watch*, the sort of cop movie she's happy to let me watch alone. "Something was going on," she says, "and not far from here." We don't pay for the apartment's cable service when we come to Los Angeles, and we always leave our computer at home, but before we go to dinner with my daughter, Shannon logs on and learns that Johnny Lewis, an actor who was in the first two seasons of *Sons of Anarchy*, has beaten his landlady to death, killed and dismembered her cat, and either fallen or jumped to his own death from the roof of a Los Feliz house.

Under the heading "Breaking News" are a few additional short sentences: "Investigators believe *Sons of Anarchy* actor Johnny Lewis killed his elderly landlord, Catherine Davis, 81. Lewis was found sprawled in the driveway.

"Did you ever watch that show?" my daughter asks.

"For five minutes once."

My wife notices the Lowry Road address of the crime scene. "That's right behind our apartment," she says. "No wonder the helicopters were over my head."

"Right behind?" I echo.

"Really close. A couple of blocks up."

*

After dinner we make our way home in the dark, and I tell my wife I want to walk up Lowry to the murder scene. "Why?" she says, and I let it go and follow her inside.

"Something always happens close when you come here," I say. "Remember the fire?"

"That's nothing like a murder. That's some place we could look at later when everything was taken care of."

Once, when my wife visited without me, she arrived the day a fire in Griffith Park spread rapidly, the smoke and ash reaching my daughter's apartment as they ate dinner. The next day they were evacuated to a motel and spent two days bunched together in one room. Six months later, we walked through the park until we reached a place where the path began to twist upward and we could see where the charred trees spread out below us, and where, on the other side of the shallow valley, untouched vegetation let us know just how close the fire had come to making the leap into the neighborhood of expensive homes set into the hillside across the street from my daughter's apartment, the same neighborhood where the landlady's murder had just occurred.

We buy a newspaper, the first time I'd picked up one since we'd been in town near the 40th anniversary date of the Manson murders. "Near Griffith Park" is how the setting is described in the article about Johnny Lewis killing his landlady. It's the same phrase used three years earlier when my daughter mentioned that the house where the less-publicized, second night of Manson murders took place was located directly above her apartment. I was surprised then, but we were leaving the next day, and I forgot about the LaBiancas and their nearby house until now, when a murder with a celebrity alleged-killer already generating a brush fire of publicity was just as markedly close.

I ask Shannon to remind me about the exact location of the LaBianca house.

"Right up the hill behind us," Shannon says, and my wife adds that I was told the same thing three years before. I let her impatience go, step outside to reconnoiter.

From my daughter's patio, the forty-three year-old events seem less remote. The distance to the top of the slope looks to be about 100 feet, but the hillside is steep enough to convince me a fall and serious injury would be likely if I chanced a climb. "There's some sort of wall up there," my daughter says when she sees me looking up. "And there are coyotes," she adds, her way of protecting me from foolishness.

"Ok," I say, "I'm not going straight up," but I tell my wife I not only want to walk to the Johnny Lewis murder site, I want to climb the street that leads to the LaBianca house.

"We're in the murder neighborhood," I say, and she frowns.

"There's something wrong with you," she says, but she agrees to go to the LaBianca house because everything happened so long ago. Even better, she knows exactly how to get there.

A few minutes later, when a loud squawking reaches us, I say to my daughter, "There goes your neighbor again. Is she crazy?"

Shannon doesn't answer until the squawking comes again. "That's the real peacock," she says.

*

"All this violence right on top of us," my wife says the next morning as we cross Los Feliz Boulevard on our way to Shannon's apartment. "But at least the homeless guy is gone."

The year before, for five months, a homeless man nested among the trees in the only hillside space without a house set into it on my daughter's street, his clothes strung upon branches like chronic laundry, shopping carts shimmering like chrome-slathered antique cars. Even when we couldn't see anyone, my wife tensed every time we walked by during that visit. Every day during the week we visited, though the squatter's space was three doors down, she told our daughter she should call the police without waiting for the residents right next to that vacant property to call.

As we round a sharp curve, a woman is standing by our daughter's steps. Though her hair is as black as her black blouse and tight black leggings, her face is heavily lined, and she looks to be, like my wife and me, in her sixties. Shannon introduces us, adding that the woman lives "right down there," and I know we're meeting the peacock caller.

She doesn't disappoint. She reports a night of coyotes, how she listened to them for hours, worrying until a half-hour ago, when she saw the peacock resting upon the gray-tiled roof of the house next to my daughter's.

"From way up there," she says, "that beauty could photograph Los Angeles." All of us look up to the empty roof. "It has to be close," the woman says. She is so fixated that I expect her to give us a squawk or two, but she goes down the steps to her apartment without working up a call.

"She used to be a makeup artist," Shannon says.

*

There's no way my wife and I can climb directly up the steep hillside, so we need to walk a half-mile loop to a street that begins to wind upward to where the houses become progressively more lavish and expensive. We follow the twists of Waverly Drive until we reach the Cardinal Timothy Manning House of Prayer for Priests, which, according to my best estimate, directly overlooks our daughter's house.

"It looks like a resort hotel for monks," I say.

The enormous property is gated, with a perimeter wall that lines the street for such a distance that I go back and step off 350 paces, guessing about 300 yards of frontage. The Spanish style buildings stretch across much of the perfectly kept grounds. The Brothers of the Good Shepherd, who apparently host other priests looking to spend time on retreat, would make a fortune if they sold this property.

"There's no chance of homeless squatters lasting more than a few minutes up here," I say.

"Right," my wife says, "but down where your daughter lives, it took months for the police to chase that guy away."

"Once they got around to it, they emptied that place of his like burglars," I say, but I'm regretting that there's no possible way to walk to the edge of the steep hill and look down on my daughter's house. I imagine an alarm system. I conjure well-trained dogs.

But it's not far to the LaBianca house. Though the street number doesn't match what I'd looked up, it unmistakably matches the photographs I examined on the Internet the day before. While I stare up the driveway from the same angle as a few of the crime scene photographs, my wife tells me that two doors down, across the street, our granddaughter attended a birthday party for a classmate earlier this year.

"Really?" I say, remembering that I'd read, once, that Manson had attended a party in the vicinity as well, that the reason the LaBianca house was chosen was the accident of his familiarity with Waverly and the isolation of the houses there.

Before I'm done marveling at the chain of coincidences, a man approaches walking a tiny, tightly-furred dog that excitedly tugs its leash until it stands right by my feet. When I reach down to give it a quick pat, the man says, "Mr. Muggles likes you."

"Looks that way," I say.

"I walk him for his owner. He's lived up here for quite some time but doesn't get out much anymore."

I can't help but estimate that "quite some time" might very well place that dog owner on this street in the summer of 1969, and the dog walker, as if reading my mind, says, "After the Manson thing, the new owners of that house changed the number of the street address. Some people come up here and get confused."

"I can understand why" is all I can manage, and with a smile, the dog walker guides Mr. Muggles away from us.

"We should be getting back," my wife says. We've agreed to walk our granddaughters and the dog back to our apartment and keep them overnight, giving my daughter a "day of rest" because her marriage has fallen apart, her husband living elsewhere. The way down wears hard on my arthritic and cartilage-missing knees.

A half-hour later, reading from my daughter's computer, I tell my wife that Johnny Lewis played a character called "Half-Sack" because he was missing a testicle. "Of course," she says, and I forego the rest of what I've learned about the scenarios of *Sons of Anarchy*. But when I read a story that describes the scene of the murder as an "artist's villa" and lists the site as in the 3600 block of Lowry Road, I say, "You're right about how close that house is to our apartment."

"Then go ahead and take a look tomorrow morning," she says. "You're the one who thinks it's interesting to look at murder sites."

"There's a house Walt Disney lived in up there behind you, too," our daughter says, but I don't react until she adds, "The story has it that the LaBiancas lived there before they moved up to Waverly."

"This is getting creepy," my wife says. She pulls out my daughter's wedding album, and the way she looks at the photos makes me believe she is looking for signs of the marriage's failure that she somehow missed on the day of the ceremony.

With my wife fixated on the photos, I turn to my daughter. "Remember when Mom got out her wedding dress for you to wear?"

119

"I wish I could have," she says, "but it wasn't in good enough shape. Mom looked beautiful in it."

Our granddaughters come out of their room with their overnight bags packed, keeping me from blurting out another case of proximity, how in one of the professional photographs taken before, during, and after our wedding, a young girl is attaching paper flowers to the car my wife and I would drive on our honeymoon. She lived next door to my wife's family and was visibly excited to be part of what was happening that August afternoon in 1968.

Thirteen years ago, shortly before my daughter was married, that girl, because she was scheduled to testify against a man accused of a crime, was murdered. The accused man broke into her house and killed her. He lived next door to her in an adjacent, refurbished row house. He'd tunneled through the wall to get to her. He'd dragged her body back through the hole in the wall and dismembered her in his basement.

Just as we all step outside, we hear the distinctive squawk, audible even over the noise of a furious surge of cars on Los Feliz as the light changes.

"The real peacock," my daughter says, though we can't make it out. "What do you think that sound it's making means?" she goes on. "Fear or loneliness?"

*

The following morning I take the dog along. It needs to exercise, and it makes me feel like I have a purpose other than rubbernecking. The drawback is the white German shepherd's excitement to be outside, how, when it tugs at the leash, my knees remind me that Lowry is as steep as Waverly, that coming back down with the dog scrambling ahead will be penance for curiosity.

If there's a yard that doesn't display a security sign, I don't see it. Half the signs have extra warnings that promise an armed response, and I take it as a suggestion, this morning, that the response would come from within.

By the time Lowry spirals up to the 3600 block murder site, the houses unmistakably "loom" on the side of the street where the crime took place, each house built for height, I imagine, to guarantee a view. The short driveways are all steep, the houses fortress-like. A few houses have pulley systems that I guess are for the luxury of delivered groceries and packages.

Nobody is outside near the murder house, but now I'm happy to have the dog on its leash because it makes me look like a resident of the neighborhood, someone who lives close by, someone who belongs there. The driveway at the murder site is pitched so steeply I can see at once how a head-first tumble from the roof or even the balcony could be fatal.

What else I'm certain of is that from an upstairs window in that house, someone could look across Los Feliz Boulevard and see my daughter's apartment.

*

That evening, when we walk our granddaughters and the dog to their house, Shannon tells us the peacock has been retrieved and returned to Griffith Park. Her neighbor, apparently, hasn't gotten the word, because we all hear her squawk what now sounds like a plaintive, impossible mating call.

On the way back to our apartment, approaching the grove of trees where the homeless man once lived, my wife says she's worried about coyotes. "I've seen them," she says, "even if you never have."

Nearing Los Feliz Boulevard, packed as always with cars and trucks and buses, I begin to limp. It is all I can do to cross the highway before the "walk" sign blinks off, and the traffic lunges forward.

A PUNISHMENT SEMINAR

The first person executed in Pennsylvania, after more than thirty years, worked at the mall just outside the small college town where I live. Keith Zettlemoyer died by lethal injection, the method deemed most humane since the last Pennsylvania execution. Certainly, it's more humane than the preceding choice of the gas chamber, which took, on occasion, ten minutes to kill. For sure, it's less grotesque than the electric chair, another recent favorite of the humane, which had its share of embarrassing moments: men charred by overdose, men reviving and then reshocked, one man alive in the chair after the power blew while the current ran through him.

So the world works to be civil while it tries to fit punishment to crime, even the small and the common. In college, during my sophomore year, I put in hours of public service to work off the sins of my fraternity brothers. "You serve as a group or two of you are expelled," the school told us, and we picked up litter, weeded, and landscaped on Saturday mornings. I felt better about myself, but I was also failing two classes, one requiring a textbook I hadn't bought and one during which I had a job and didn't attend except to take the three exams, the last two of which I failed.

I was put on academic probation and threatened with dismissal, the capital punishment of academia, and then summer set in, months of factory work during which I sweated near steaming vats of prepared soup for the Heinz Company on the North Side of Pittsburgh. And those days I didn't lift and carry, I assisted in sterilizing, the hottest work site in the factory, counting the days until I could return to the lighter sentence of regularly attending class and turning in required work on time.

I wasn't far wrong in imagining my work in sterilizing as capital punishment. Boiling was once, in fact, a form of execution. Not for long (sixteen years in England during the sixteenth century), but it had its run at trying to frighten people from their evil ways. The first person executed this way, ironically, was a cook. He was lowered into a pot and the fire built up beneath it. The watched pot, the inefficient fire, the weak conduction of the special container—whatever the reason, that cook required a long time to succumb, lasting two hours in that slowly heating broth.

How long before the cook's initial terror settled into tepid resignation? He was simmering because he'd been convicted of attempting to poison, though the punishment, according to all accounts, wasn't designed to fit his crime any more than the punishment meted out by the man, more recently, who shot his wife for too often serving beans. "Wouldn't you be mad?" he said to the police, as if all of us might form lines to shoot, remembering carrots and oatmeal, liver, sauerkraut, and whatever else might be added to a list of avoidable hates.

And there are others who are equally angry, administering punishments like the Pittsburgh banker who spanked customers late with their loan repayments, a crude version of one sergeant's technique, building human xylophones with his new recruits, assigning each with a note to sing when he was pummeled with a bat.

And there are those who punish like the exasperated teacher who rewarded her good students by having them spit on the bad, citing a history of such punishments devised by her predecessors.

*

"What's so funny?" my tenth grade homeroom teacher demanded once, keeping me after opening exercises.

"Nothing," I said, relying on the usual answer to release me to first period Latin II.

The rest of the students filed out, but this teacher wouldn't let it go, my smiling during the Bible reading. "You think there's no God?" he said. "That it? You laughing at God? Go ahead, say it, say there's no God." He grabbed my wrists, held them up in front of my face like a primitive polygraph, but I kept my eyes on the knot in his tie, this homeroom teacher who mispronounced so badly, reading adult-airy that morning from Chronicles.

He breathed cigarettes and coffee into my suspect's face. The bell rang, and thirty general math students bunched near the doorway, not one of them coming inside to hear what I had to say about the meaning of life, whether or not opening exercises mattered.

It was the year before the Supreme Court took the Bible out of his hands, but he leaned in so close, repeating, "Say there's no God and go to hell. Say it," that I repeated cavalry, tabranaclee, seplacher to myself, lip-sealed and breathing through my nose, what I could keep doing, alone, until he wrote my pass to the office where the principal would see to it that I spent a week in the auditorium after school to think about the consequences of my disbelief.

Twenty-six years later, my son and two friends, fifteen years old on a tenth-grade field trip, order beer with their lunch at the Smithsonian Institute. Incredibly, they are served. Miraculously, a woman visiting the same day from our town recognizes them and reports their names, the following day, to the principal.

One boy confesses, and all three are suspended for ten days. I take my son with me for a meeting with the principal and the teacher who took the students to Washington. I ask why the students, none of them as old as sixteen, were unsupervised for six hours. "We've never had a problem before," the teacher says, using the logic of the absentee landlord.

124

When I ask why an older boy, suspended the same day for underage drinking within a mile of the high school, is being allowed to star in the senior class play and attend the prom though my son cannot play in his scheduled tennis matches, the principal says, "It's because the play and the prom are once-in-a-lifetime opportunities" this time using logic resembling the English law that made suicide a capital crime.

Surely that was an incentive to do things right the first time. Three stories up, you would climb an extra flight of stairs to be sure. Five miles from shore, you would wait another five miles before you leapt overboard. Or you would reposition that gun, calculate carefully, because failure permitted someone else to do it for you, or, most likely in England at that time, position a noose around your neck.

"He that is hanged is accursed by God," it says in Deuteronomy, accounting, perhaps, for its popularity with the church, but for years medical and scientific experts as well debated the possibility of achieving the clean hang, the perfect execution, the neck of the criminal snapped each time, not the victim slowly strangling while he dangled above the audience, not the victim's head nearly or even completely torn off because he'd plunged too far.

Early in the debate came the question of knots—which to use, where to place it. There were advocates for behind-the-ear, supporters for the nape of the neck and just underneath the Adam's apple.

And there were years spent testing the rope length and the drop distance, evaluating the results of varying combinations.

Doctors became consultants. They debated the punishment research, argued the data of the long drop and filed their reports in professional journals with column after column of requisite graphs: distance versus the variables of neck size, weight, thickness of the noose. And finally, the cult of the rope choice arose, fanatics for particular weaves, for places of origin, for whether or not to pre-stretch.

And marketing? The rope as souvenir, snipped into pieces for the clean-hang collectors. Last interviews with the convicted were published in limited editions.   People wanted to know what tongues with nothing to lose might utter—blasphemy, scatological curses, sentences straightforward with colorful rage just before the collar was arranged, the hair delicately lifted.

As it turned out, in those journals of the hanging cart, nearly always the victims lamented their life's misdeeds, a surprise, perhaps, except that these regrets were most often ghost-written by ministers or priests as a sort of Extra for God's newspaper, illustrated, moreover, with eyewitness drawings: the raised eyes of the just-converted, mothers of criminals blowing kisses to their children, and one appearance, on the scaffold, by the Holy Ghost shown standing near the repentant felon who's been examined for weight, for the muscle thickness of his calipered neck, his head thrust through a carefully chosen rope tied by an expert knot, his drop height calculated, all of those statistics arriving at a personalized formula for death.

*

In the room beside mine during my probation semester in college, a fraternity brother kept an arsenal. He had handguns and rifles, and one weekend, drunk, he stood in the back doorway and shot out the lights in the parking lot, bringing a security car to investigate.

Nobody in the house said anything, another example of fraternity loyalty, but one night I rode home with him from Youngstown, Ohio, most of the trip at over 100 miles per hour so, he told me, I would know you could survive excessive speed on well-travelled roads. "See?" he said, parking, and I nodded, but he destroyed that Thunderbird and another before the third one buckled back in a head-on to shear his legs at the knees.

"See?" I might have said, meaning denouement, meaning I'd learned one answer for the tearing of the bone's lace. That semester I also learned beheading was considered more humane than hanging. In another class I read Chaucer and discovered the purpose of Pardoners, how donations to the church might lessen one's eternal sentencing, but I said nothing, after the crippling accident, about the possible reason for partial punishment.

126

And I've learned, since then, that fairy tales, the originals at least, rely on such punishments severe and swift and graphic. Goldilocks, for instance, who in the earliest version is gray-haired and thin, homeless, and angry. The three bears have left milk behind, and the old crone finds it sour, contenting herself with settling in to sleep in a comfortable bed.

Those bears, when they come home, are unhappy. They don't want vagrants in their house; they want justice, and they toss Goldilocks into the fire, and, when she doesn't broil, sink her in water. She resurfaces, still alive, and the bears, desperate, take her to St. Paul's Cathedral and skewer her on the steeple, which, at least in this version, successfully finishes her.

Self-punishment was brutal, too, as in Cinderella, where the stepsisters snip off their toes and part of their heels to wedge themselves into the slipper. "When you are queen, you won't have to walk anymore," their mother tells them, but they can't quite make an exact match. So they limp, then use crutches. So they're carried, eventually, downstairs to the fitting, and at the end of this story, their eyes are torn out by the beaks of doves, the punishment for vanity and shame.

In the original Sleeping Beauty, the Prince rapes her when he believes her dead. So of course he doesn't stay, but leaves Beauty pregnant in her coma to bear twins while sleeping. It's her son who sucks the splinter from her thumb, rouses her just in time to face the Prince who's returned for another easy lay.

She's already been established as a miracle by the time he arrives, and astonished, he confesses. More astonishing, she welcomes him back, though not yet happily ever after, since the prince is married to a woman who doesn't forgive. The wife has punishment on her mind and cooks those twins as the main ingredient in her husband's hash. As usual, he gobbles his dinner, but when, triumphant, she tells him that he's eaten his children, she learns that the cook has cheated, substituted goat for babies like the chef of loud conscience. "Won't anybody be true?" she thinks, and takes over punishment herself, binds Beauty to the bonfire stake just before she's rescued, of course, by the Prince because she's somebody to return to, because by now he relies upon her easy love.

*

My daughter, at nineteen, attracted stalkers. One called each night, drunk and remorseful until, after a few weeks, he turned drunk and bitter. I knew his voice; he'd stood in my kitchen beside her. Now, my daughter recently moved out, he wanted her phone number and her address, asking me to intercede.

That summer, when she came home from college, a man followed her through the mall. He ate pretzels from Hot Sam and watched her sell shoes. Finally, he entered the store, sat in a chair, having her slide off his sneakers to fit him, one size, then another, then a third before he said "sorry" and followed her, an hour later, toward her car, which she passed, three slots to its right, angling back to the open door of the drug store to call me.

I considered the punishments I wanted to mete out to that man, the eye for an eye of pursuing him in my car until he parked where I could follow, so obvious and so close behind him his lips would begin to part and move, his brain sending signals to his nerve endings that might accelerate his feet or suggest he defend himself.

Sitting on my deck that summer, I told a friend about my fantasy, how stalking deserved restalking, how I'd researched capital punishment, discovering the earliest recorded method in Europe was throwing the criminal into a quagmire. "For terror," I said, "and economy."

For my birthday, as he had for years, this friend wrapped the worst beer he could find. He'd had a year to do more research, and some of those twenty-four bottle cases spent months in my kitchen, evidence enough of his meticulous scholarship for swill.

"In Babylonia," I told him, "selling bad beer was a capital crime," and we laughed while we recalled the roster of the dreadful—Shakespeare, America's Best, the no-name generic from another state where you can pull the beer off grocery shelves.

"Jesus Christ," he said, and I offered, "In Judea, people were put to death for cursing; in Assyria, for giving bad haircuts; in Rome, for making disturbances at night."

I could have gone on, having learned that people had been executed for injuring cats and slaughtering cows. And the Babylonians again, who put to death the architect if the house fell on its owner or, if it collapsed on the owner's son, put the architect's son to death. The logic of an eye for an eye had its limits, though, because if the house fell on the owner's wife or daughters, the architect was fined. Neither I nor my friend, nostalgic, finally, with beer and my birthday, admitted to anything but living inside houses where photographs traced us backwards like Darwin's evidence, sweet traits which might save us, fit for the pleasures of clemency.

SELF-DEFENSE

1

In a nearby town, late at night, a woman plays her stereo louder and longer than her neighbors can bear. At last, they call the police.

The woman who has cranked three hours of CDs is drunk and uncooperative, no surprise to the police, but she also owns snakes, and when the police enter her home, intending to subdue her, she uses them as a weapon, hissing "Back off" as she brandishes her copperheads, two in each hand, like automatic weapons.

The situation becomes a standoff. They were responding to a simple disturbing the peace complaint, but now the two policemen keep their distance for a curse-filled half hour.

Other police arrive. The call's description of the stalemate has made them curious about this spin-off of the Medusa story, and finally the room is dotted with uniforms.

Though religion isn't a force in that room, the woman repeating blasphemies, she has the faith of those churchgoers who decide which of them is saved by their ease with snakes. Her pets, naturally, are leery of the small congregation of law.

Finally, she's bitten, and more than once. She disarms herself by dropping the snakes back under glass. "It wasn't surrender," she's quoted in our local newspaper's next day account. "Just a truce."

"You own snakes like mine, you learn your poisons," she says. "I knew I could still be saved by anybody trained to deal with snake venom, and those cops, they listened to me as if they'd accidentally shot me."

One of those policemen agreed that even with that woman reduced from criminal to patient, he, at least, kept a space between himself and her as if she might lunge and strike. "Self-defense," the woman says. "That's all it was I was doing."

2

For self-defense, my mother recommended the power of positive thinking. Until I reached sixth grade, she read passages to me from books and magazines about believing in myself, how it improved the immune system of both the body and the mind, keeping sickness and sin at bay.

"Don't you forget," my mother would say, "headaches are no worse than pimples. Find yourself something to do. Forget the pain." She worked and drank coffee to subdue hers, swallowing the home treatments of busyness and caffeine.

At my grandmother's house, in the living room where there was a television, something we didn't own during that time, my mother arranged chairs from the kitchen like three pieces of a straight-backed pew. My sister and I filed in behind her with reverence because on Sunday nights Bishop Fulton Sheen would take half an hour to improve us.

"Life is worth living," he repeated, sounding just like the minister I'd listened to nine hours earlier. Like a teacher, he wrote words and phrases on a blackboard: Self-confidence breeds self-improvement; eternal success is heaven's joy.

Didn't I see, my mother would say, that the best self-defense was faith? That I could influence eternity by heeding Christ? When I closed my eyes I saw the shows my friends had told me I was missing on other channels. While Bishop Sheen flourished his robed arms into a brief drama of blessing, I thought of the bus ride to school the following morning, the chatter of my friends, and how I would look out the window as if anything that might be seen along Route 8 was more interesting than a summary of jokes and crime-solving from the night before.

3

In 1957, when I was eleven years old, the army produced *The Big Picture*, a program for television to lessen the fears of the public about nuclear explosions. My family owned a television now, and my mother, my sister, and I watched.

The Big Picture unrolled like the foot-wide group photograph I received at the end of my stay at Camp Lutherlyn each summer. The narrator said dusk on the desert is a reflective time, this particular evening, perhaps, a bit more full of deep thinking than most. He said an awesome power was ready and able, but in the minds of some men, fundamental questions remained.

The Big Picture showed us a chaplain who preached the gospel of a fireball ascending into heaven. It listened as he said the cloud had all the rainbow's rich colors before it turned into a beautiful pale yellow mushroom.

The Big Picture silenced us and held our breath. The screen turned so bright I remembered trying to stare at the sun.

The Big Picture argued that an acceptable answer for the question of safety near the blast was wearing regular clothes. The army wanted men exposed to the pressure of a forced, post-blast march, and the camera followed those men to Ground Zero while a voice assured us the soldiers were adequately informed.

The Big Picture went to commercial when the men lost composure. The narrator stayed mum about terror. Like Jesus, he insisted we needn't be afraid.

4

Because my father has declared, more than once, that using an inhaler was something the weak did, the first time I used one I heard him criticizing, decades ago, a boy who wheezed in church until he was led, at last, from a front pew by his mother's hand. "Like a Little Lord Fauntleroy," he'd said with such contempt that I didn't ask him who that was.

I could see Sylvia Rogers at the dance she invited me to in eighth grade, her pale skin and her beige-colored inhaler, the first I ever saw someone use. She made me think of the girls Poe wrote about, the beauty of someone young and vulnerable. My father, when I recounted the evening, said nobody, as Sylvia had told me about herself, could be allergic to dust. "How could you live?" he said. "It's everywhere, like air."

Because my own three children were young when I had my first asthma emergency, a nightlight was on in the bathroom where I stood holding the plastic tube like a handgun I might press against my temple. My breath whistled its warning, yet I spent another minute examining my dim self in the mirror to mark who I'd become at thirty-eight, someone who relied on medicine for self-defense, someone ashamed of his dependence.

At last, I inhaled that mist, holding it in my lungs, repeating the dose twice for relief. I walked bare-footed through the drawn-drape darkness of my living room, daring the furniture to be out of place or toys scattered like tacks on the floor. I could hear my father repeating "Sick days" like a synonym for shit. I believed my future, now, was warm and small, waiting in a thicket for darkness because there was nothing worse than admitting weakness.

5

About that same time, a swarm of ants somehow materialized on the counter by our kitchen sink at a time when my parents were visiting. My mother said she would explain, "Just this once, so listen," giving advice on keeping ants at bay:

"It's too late now, but you need to know that ants are allergic to cucumbers. Bits of skin will keep clear the places where they swarm."

She wasn't finished. "It's too late now," she went on, "but ants hate chalk. They won't cross a thick line of it if you draw a circle around something edible that you love."

The ants multiplied as she talked. I thought she enjoyed confirming whatever helplessness she saw in me because of their presence. "A little lemon juice can be a moat," she said. "You can soak your doorway and the window sills."

Finally, she poured a tablespoon of sugar into a cup of water, stirred it, and soaked a sponge in the solution. "Let's leave it on this plate you already left out here," she said, "while I heat some water. It won't be long before those ants congregate like pigs. See? Let them do exactly that before you use some tongs—you have some, don't you? — to pick up that sponge and plunge it into the boiling water."

We massacred those ants. We nearly wiped them out with one good dunk, but she kept on. "You're not finished. Wash that sponge out and wring it hard. Begin again. There's always stragglers."

At last there were only two or three, and she rubbed them out with her thumb. "You know what ants are good for?" she said. "They point out peoples' carelessness, a crowd of them teeming where dessert was dropped, a bit so tiny some people don't bend for it. Something like pennies on the sidewalk, so little to be gained some people leave them like litter. Think about that. And make sure you don't forget these old remedies I'm handing down. The ants will stay outside where they belong."

6

Like oatmeal, spinach and bread crusts, blunt talk put hair on your chest and grew the muscles you needed to defend yourself and take care of business. It separated heroes from pussies, and Coach Czak used it like an open hand, clapping boys who took a charge on the back, saying "Hell, yes," to the players who earned floor burns diving for loose balls.

Blunt talk was Coach Czak saying, "Having that time of the month?" when someone tired. He was getting us ready for the world or the army where, either way, blunt talk would show us exactly where we stood.

In business, the hesitant were faggots; in Vietnam, the cowardly were cunts. The 60s were ripe, but we weren't, not yet, and Coach Czak would help us grow. "Just wait," he promised, "when we're finished here, you'll all be different," and we were, clearing our throats for the first barrage of blunt talk, trying it out on the weak and quiet, ready to work our way up like boxers, ready to be serious contenders.

7

Once, the father of a girl I was dating led me outside of the house he owned that had four times the floor space of my parents' house to explain the advantages of natural security. "Some people plant mint because it releases a powerful smell when stepped on by anybody who's trespassing," he said. "That doesn't cut it with me, but some get the idea better when they put beehives along their borders," making me understand that the gated driveway was the only acceptable entrance.
He told me there were 4.7 acres he could call his own. He showed me around, describing what belonged to him, and guided me, finally, toward what I took to be the outermost edge of his property because there was a wall of head-high hedges. "Touch these," he said, showing me the stiletto thorns. "Look how thick," he said, and I took his word, seeing nothing beyond the tightly clustered leaves and branches.

"People who need protection should look into this stuff," he said. "It's called trifoliate orange, and it grows to twenty feet if you let it, a wall so thick it stops a jeep."

I touched one four-inch spike and didn't mention the time, when, eleven years-old and running after dark, I sprawled, hands flailing, into the ordinary waist-high hedge of a neighbor. I had scratches but nothing near my eyes, a sprained ankle, but not a shattered leg. And I had time, lying there, to note the wire strung calf-high a foot from that well-maintained hedge, as if whoever lived behind it and its sparse, small thorns expected boys like me to run through his bushes, as if he owned a country so valuable there were invaders perpetually ready to cross that border.

8

The one time I hitchhiked with a girl we were offered rides more quickly than I'd ever received them on my own. I was in graduate school. She was eighteen, a freshman, who I'd told over a pitcher of the 3.2 beer she could legally drink in Ohio, that hitching was the way I got back and forth to Pittsburgh where, by coincidence, she had a boyfriend she wanted to see.

Returning from our weekend trip, it had taken six rides to approach Columbus, so it was a relief when, as twilight settled in and we climbed into the back of a car, that the two men in the front seat said they were going to Kentucky, meaning this ride would take us almost a hundred miles and leave us at an exit less than half an hour from Oxford.

I relaxed and watched the landscape turn rural as it rolled by in the gathering darkness. After it became too dark to see much of anything off to the side, I began to drift until the radio skidded up to near roar level. I sat up, recognizing Led Zeppelin just as the driver jerked his head around and said, "Fucking great shit."

I nodded, but the girl I was with suddenly looked apprehensive, as if the radio's volume signaled something threatening, and for the first time I calculated the difference between one man and two in the front seat of a strange car.

When the Zeppelin song ended, the car began to slow, and a moment later we were rolling onto an exit ramp that looked remote, not even a gas station waiting near the upcoming stop sign. "What's out here?" I managed to croak.

The driver swiveled almost completely, and this time, grinning, he said, "Dinner. The best hamburger you'll ever eat."

He rolled through the stop sign, accelerating at once onto a two-lane that twisted into forest. "Pictures of Lily," a song by The Who that was supposed to be about masturbation came on, but I searched along the floor with my shoes, hoping to touch something heavy and hard. I needed a weapon, and that car was immaculate with emptiness. The fingers of the girl's right hand dug into my thigh. She was staring over the driver's shoulder, reading, I imagined, the speedometer for the first small increment of deceleration.

The thought came to me that these guys might shoot me before they raped and strangled that girl. My next thought was that there would be a moment as the car slowed down when that girl and I could open our respective doors and throw ourselves out, getting to our feet and running. That might save me, but I couldn't imagine the girl outrunning them.

The woods thickened, trees running right down to the shoulder. Before long, I became certain there would be a dirt road turning off, and I'd know where I was going to die. I searched along the floor with my hand as if something valuable had escaped the notice of my shoe. I wondered if she carried a curling iron in her small, overnight bag that sat on the seat between us, whether my set of three keys might be fashioned into a weapon.

"Eight Miles High" came on the radio, the Byrds at speaker-threatening volume. I had the record in my apartment. The guy in the shotgun seat turned and stared back at us so pointedly that the girl brought her arms up in front of her breasts. "Isn't this the greatest fucking song ever?" the man said.

I saw a break in the woods, a turn off, and I braced myself, watching for what would be in the man's hand when he lifted it higher than the back of the seat. The car slowed. I could hear the girl's breathing as she strangled my thigh. I tried to focus.

And then the car drifted by the turn off, rounding a bend to where a diner sat back off the road within a grove of trees. The driver pulled in and said, "Here we are," leaving the motor run until the Byrds were finished. "Perfect," the shotgun seat man said. "Fucking perfect."

I had to agree. I was as happy as I'd ever been, and I climbed out and followed them, pausing only when I was in the doorway to look back to where the girl stood near the car like a small child who'd been hoping for McDonald's.

The driver waved her on. The three of us waited until she walked toward us. Fifteen minutes later I was relaxed over what proved to be an excellent hamburger complete with cheese, tomatoes, onions, and lettuce.

When we finally arrived in Oxford, that girl didn't say anything except "Do you remember what those men looked like or what they were wearing?"

I was quiet for a moment as she slapped the overnight bag against the side of her leg. "No," I said. I could name every song that played on the radio and what both men had ordered on their hamburgers, but I didn't remember anything about them except they were clean-shaven and white.

"You acted like you were happy while you were eating," she said. "What did you think, that those guys were our friends?" Her look let me know she'd decided I was a fool. As she walked into her dorm, her tight jeans made me remember the exact shape of her thighs and hips. I never saw her again.

9

My mother died twenty-five years ago. My father, a few years later, gave in to heart surgery. Several years after that, he surrendered to a cane and then, needing a walker, he was embarrassed to be seen in public for the last five years of his life.

This morning I read the instructions for how to rid your house of ghosts. To begin, it said, politely, but firmly, ask them to leave. They're not to blame for loitering. Convince each one that the physical world is no place to hide from elder spirits who will, with time, forgive their sins.

The ghosts of your family are docile except those who died young. Naturally, they are quick to anger. Don't you be angry, too. They'll feed on it. Likewise, don't show fear. Ghosts smell opportunity in weakness.

Listen, there's reason for their restlessness. You may have outlived some of the ones you know by fifty years, so they're rightfully sick of your breathing and the terrible leisure of language. All your healthy days are enough to anger anyone, but they know that safety is as tenuous as cupping the groin against fists and knees. When it comes to ridding yourself of them, what matters is believing in the self–defense of truth.

THOREAU'S CANE

Henry Thoreau, years before he spent his famous time at Walden Pond, was a schoolteacher. Not very long after beginning his tenure, he was told by a school committee member that in order to keep students under control, regular canings were expected. Because he'd been reprimanded for being too lenient, Thoreau began more often to strike the open palms of his students with the cane supplied by the school until, one afternoon, he resigned rather than continue such routine, approved corporal punishment.

The first time I laid a hand on one of my ninth grade students during my first year of teaching English in 1968, the victim was a girl who sat in the front row, her desk flush against mine. One afternoon, before I began to read off questions for a quiz, a boy walked up and used the pencil sharpener that was bolted to the desk. A second boy strolled forward and carefully sharpened his pencil as everyone watched. A third followed suit.

A moment later, when the girl in the front desk leaned forward and pushed her pencil into the sharpener, I grabbed her wrist and twisted, the pencil snapping in half. She sat stunned as I began to read off the questions. Without a pencil and without anyone nearby offering her one, she was unable to write the answers. The class was quiet while I collected their answer sheets. She never complained about her F.

Almost always, even when corporal punishment in schools was common and even expected, it was forbidden for use on girls. Girls were different from boys. It was thought by many school authorities that they would be scarred for life rather than improved.

"Shhhh" Miss Effington, the school librarian would say. "Shhhh," she would repeat a few minutes later. I was in seventh grade, new to being set free in a library to read independently for forty-five minutes at a time. "Shhhhh," Miss Effington said again and again until one day she latched on to a boy's shoulders with both hands and shook him hard. He was sitting in the chair next to me, and I believed my turn might be next. Everyone got quiet.

"A good shaking is what all of you need," she hissed at the boys at my table. "Know-it-alls," she said, standing so close to me as she kept her hands hooked into his shoulders that I could barely see past her dark blue dress.

Miss Effington glared at all of us. "Keep it up," she said, "and you'll get just what the doctor ordered." A minute later, back behind her desk, she said "Shhhh."

Quintillian, during the first century A.D., made a case against corporal punishment because it was a disgrace and that it would ultimately harden the boy being punished. "How will that boy be treated as a man?" was the question he posed.

During my three years in junior high school, grades seven through nine, students were often paddled. They were always boys, and in the three classes I had where that happened immediately after such offenses as talking back, disturbing the class, or failing to heed multiple warnings about chewing gum, the student was given the opportunity to sign the paddle, a privilege many of the punished thought was so "cool" they bragged about the number of signatures they'd written.

Once, my seventh grade math teacher told Al Voyteck and me to see him after school. He'd had enough of our horseplay, and it was a short walk from his classroom to the locker room where the junior high football coach kept a paddle in his office. "It's about time," he said, but when we arrived, the door was locked, and instead of paddling us, he said, "This is your lucky day" and both of us scrambled out the back door of the school into the late afternoon sunshine.

Plutarch, during the first century, echoed Quintillian's opinion. Praise incites boys toward what is honorable, he declared. When coupled with reproof to keep them from what is disgraceful, he thought to add.

It turned out that I was never struck by an "official" paddle, but when I was a sophomore, my Latin II teacher hit me over the head with his copy of Caesar's *Gallic Wars* because I'd torn a page in a textbook as I tried to retrieve my translation from where the student across from me had stuffed it as a joke.

A few weeks later, Miss Pontius slapped my back with her teacher's edition of our English anthology for shouting out the window at a friend who was standing outside during his lunch period. Most of the class laughed.

When I was a junior in high school, a shop teacher hit a senior boy for doing the limbo in the hall where students held a broomstick and chanted "lower now" like Chubby Checker did on his latest record, adding one more dance to his repertoire of The Twist and The Fly and The Pony. There was grumbling among students, a rumor about how that boy's parents had demanded an apology, but nothing public materialized.

Near the end of that school year the principal kneed a friend of mine in the back for mocking the shuffle step seniors had to practice for the "Pomp and Circumstance" graduation entrance walk. Another friend and I waited until the principal stomped away before we laughed at the victim. Later still, we talked about how we believed the principal had lost his mind, whether you could get somebody fired for administering something like the proverbial "kick in the pants."

In 1866, in the United States a teacher struck a child nearly twenty times with a whip. People took notice.

The second time I laid a hand on a student during that first year of teaching, it was a boy who, even after several warnings, kept opening and closing my grade book while students filed into my home room as school began. I grabbed his arm and flung him away from my desk. Struggling to keep his balance, he stumbled backward through the open door and against the opposite wall in the hall.

He was an 8th grader, thirteen years old, and as surprised as I was at how easily he could be moved. Instead of complaining, he seemed to adore me after that. He greeted me every morning. He said he hoped he would be in my English class the following year. Once, when he stayed for remedial work, I gave him a ride home after school. He thanked me politely, but I never did that again after my wife reminded me that even though it was out of kindness, I could be fired for providing that ride.

At the end of the in-service day that preceded the start of my first year of teaching, the principal of the school, which housed grades seven through twelve in one large building, made a point of finding me. He wanted me to know that if I had any doubts about discipline, I should ask Miss Baker, whose room was across the hall from mine. "She's been here a very long time," he said. "She'll know what to tell you."

Whether he told Miss Baker he'd given that advice to me or not, by the end of the first week of school she showed me the paddle she kept on display in the chalk trough for the front blackboard. "You want to borrow this, it's yours any time," she said. "If you don't have the gumption to use it, send the little criminals to me, and I'll do it for you." She taught seventh grade arithmetic.

Once, in 1860, in England, a student named Reginald Cancellor was killed by his schoolmaster while being punished.

Miss Baker and another teacher named Mrs. Brownhill shared with me the same free last period of the day, and nearly every afternoon we were the only ones who sat in the no smoking faculty lounge. "Tell this new fellow how your husband handles discipline," she said one day, and after a small protest, Mrs. Brownhill told me how her husband, on the first day of school for the past twenty-five years, stood in front of every business math and algebra class he taught, took off his sport coat, rolled up his sleeves, and challenged anyone in the class who didn't want to obey him 100% of the time to come up and take his best shot.

"Twenty-five years," Mrs. Brownhill said. "It takes its toll. He has an ulcer and a heart attack to show for it."

Miss Baker looked at me. "Don't let her pooh-pooh what he's done. Not one boy has ever so much as said a peep."

I nodded because now I understood why, just a few days before when I'd entered from the back of the auditorium with her husband to help monitor an assembly, the rows of students on our half of the room had quieted from back to front as we passed down the side aisle. Not a peep. Not even when we were ten or fifteen rows away.

There is a second version of the story of Thoreau's cane. According to this one, Thoreau, after being often reprimanded for his leniency, chose six students at random and used his school-issued cane to flog each of them to show the school committee he could mete out his share of punishment. Then he abruptly resigned.

The third time I laid a hand on a student, it was March, and from behind me a boy was yelling my name, calling "Fincke" in a sarcastic way as I walked down a crowded hall with Alex Capra, another teacher, just after lunch. "Fiiiincke?" The boy's voice drew out my name into a question while Alex Capra stopped talking and seemed to be holding his breath.

The voice shouted my name six times before I pivoted and took four quick strides, picking out, between two troublemakers from one of my classes, a boy I didn't recognize in mid-"Fiiiincke?" I grabbed the boy's shirt with both hands and shoved him hard into the wall. The back of his head smacked into the cinderblock with a frightening thunk, but he recovered and swung his fist at me as I held him at arm's length. The roundhouse caught my tie and pulled it from the clip I wore. Without trying to free himself for better leverage, he swung a second time, but I was taller and had a longer reach, and then he seemed to give up, and I shifted my grip to his shoulders and turned him.

The two boys I knew were staring, and a cluster of other students had formed a horseshoe around the scene, but I pushed the boy through the crowd and guided him down the hall toward the principal's office. "Take it easy," I said, and to my surprise, he did, not struggling at all. As we neared the office and I sensed he wasn't going to turn and fight or even try to run away, I asked him what his name was.

"Gary," he said, his tone so flat I knew he wasn't mocking me. "I don't even know you," he added.

I was due in class in less than a minute, but the principal wasn't in.

"Just leave him," the secretary said at once. "I'll keep an eye on him," and without any other discussion, I hurried away.

In 1783, Poland was the first country to abolish corporal punishment.

I met my two afternoon classes with one eye on the door, but when I entered the no-smoking teacher's lounge to settle into my free period, Miss Baker said, "The talk of the town is here," and followed that line with a brief cackle.

Word had gotten around about what I'd done, and now Mrs. Brownhill offered, "We all have our breaking points."

Miss Baker beamed. "Go ahead, Sue," she said. "Tell him your story. It's a doozy."

Mrs. Brownhill took a breath and looked at me. "All these years, and the only time I completely lost my head was when this little black boy started dancing in the aisle instead of sitting down. 'What are you doing?' I asked him, and he answered 'Doing the Mashed Potato' and kept it up, and then before I knew it I grabbed him so hard he fell over backwards with me right on top, and there I was kneeling on his arms and slapping the James Brown right out of him."

"And she never had another problem with that one," Miss Baker added. Mrs. Brownhill shook her head. "Such a small thing," she said. "You

144

never know."

"You tell them and you tell them," Miss Baker said, "and then you don't."

Corporal punishment remained commonplace in England and the US into the 1980s. In 1977 the United States Supreme Court decided that paddling in public schools is lawful where it has not been specifically banned by local authorities. It remains legal in about a third of the states.

I walked to my room a few minutes before the dismissal bell and stood outside the door listening to the orderly discussion of an eighth grade history class. When the bell rang, I walked in at once, and the teacher gave me a brief look as he gathered his books before leaving with his students.

The room empty, I sat at my desk. I expected to be more than warned, some sort of discipline necessary. I began to consider possible consequences, the domino effect that would happen if I lost my job. How I'd lose my teaching deferment, how, in early 1969 and twenty-three years-old, it wouldn't be long before I'd be drafted and shipped off to Vietnam.

Teachers were required to stay in the building twenty-five minutes past the final bell, and just as twenty of those minutes had crawled by, the principal walked into my room and closed the door behind him.

"Sometimes," he began, "there are things students do or say you just can't abide, things you can't let pass." He paused, and I waited for "however" to take us into punishment.

"Alex Capra was waiting in my office when I got back. He spoke with me before I had a talk with that boy Gary Hallston you brought in. He said he wanted to explain what he'd seen and heard as best he could before everything played out."

The principal, a man who had told me in my January semi-annual evaluation that he had stood outside my door on three different occasions to hear whether or not I was in control of my classes, turned the anthology lying on my desk around as if he was about to pick it up and read something. Finally, he looked at me and said, "That boy has been suspended." He then added, "You should know that Gary Hallston comes from a troubled family, but he knows enough to keep his distance. Let's move on."

And then he turned and left, leaving the door open so Miss Baker could give me a look from her doorway. "It's ok," I said.

She nodded and said, "Good for you."

Three weeks later, Gary Hallston turned sixteen and quit school. I never heard another word about the incident, able to go on and talk about grammar or poetry or even the history of popular dances, ending with the Popcorn, the newest one my ninth graders were learning that spring from listening to James Brown, one they could climb out of their desks to demonstrate if I told them to as I began to sing.

THE SIMPLE RHYMES OF DEFENSE

Lee Pierce looked like he knew his way around. When he stopped to speak to the guard at the initial Western Penitentiary checkpoint, Pierce told him who we were instead of requesting directions. "The Scared Straight basketball team," my office mate voice-overed, citing a show that had made a small stir a few years before. "I'm pretty sure we're all going to change our ways after this."

A couple of guys laughed, but I didn't. I was uneasy already, coming to play basketball at what I knew was a prison for men who'd committed more serious crimes than DUI and delinquent child support, what accounted for most of the population in the county lockup where we all lived thirty miles north. Pierce, who coached the team at our two-year campus, had thought it would be an interesting way to spend a Sunday afternoon in early February. "What else do you have to do now that the Super Bowl is over?" he'd said.

We crossed from one gate to another, cutting through a field of dirt packed so hard it wasn't even muddy at a time of year when my yard was sopping wet from melting snow. It could have been mistaken for a parking lot if there weren't goalposts. "No pads allowed," my office mate said, keeping up his patter. He had a PhD in geology but mostly taught geography at our two-year campus, a course designed for would-be teachers that included a test that asked them to fill in the names of all the states on an otherwise blank map. "No helmets," he kept on. "The Gerald Ford bulldogs." I was hoping he'd shut up before we encountered our first prisoner.

By the time we reached the prison locker room, I had shown my comb and keys to four men and had heard three gates slam exactly as if the guards believed we were a team hired by mobsters to initiate an escape. Because my contact lens case had only been opened twice, I estimated it was half as difficult to smuggle dope as it was to transport weapons, but I kept that observation to myself.

The locker room had a bus station men's room aura that hurried all of us into our gear. "How many diseases can you catch from a toilet seat?" my office mate asked, but this time nobody laughed or even offered a guess, and I was pleased.

Pierce had brought along one non-faculty player, an associate degree student who looked to be in his mid-twenties and in shape. I didn't mind having somebody who would hustle back on defense once my legs were gone. And I especially was glad the other phys-ed professor besides Pierce was a former lineman at West Virginia, somebody with the bulk and the instincts to clear out the lane and rebound no matter what sort of men were on the other team.

Not a bad pick-up team for a bunch of professors. I'd once been a second-string college player, and Pierce had played college games when the score was close enough to make his contributions matter. Even the first guy off the bench, a math professor, had played small college ball, and he was all about hustle, slapping wrists and tugging jerseys and diving to the floor for loose balls. But that was it. The other three guys who'd made the trip were standard-order college faculty talent, guys who picked up their dribble as soon as the defense showed up, who led with their eyes when they passed, who shot and watched the result while their men released and cherry-picked for layups. Worse, none of them could run half as long as I could.

As soon as we entered the gym, I fixed on the fan-shaped iron backboards. I hadn't played at baskets like these since I'd been too small to shoot anything from outside the foul line and was at home on the grade school playground. It looked to me as if a short jump shot meant to kiss high off glass would miss this armor and land on the support. I lofted a twelve-footer and sure enough, I hit the edge. I shot from fifteen feet along the base line and produced an air ball in front of the rim. Pierce didn't seem to notice my anxiety or that of anyone else. He was excited, slapping our backs and chasing loose balls. I thought he might be using this afternoon game as a way of putting aside the nine-game losing streak his team was in the midst of.

I was glad the gym was empty except for two guards. I had time, maybe, to get acclimated. One thing I didn't have to worry about was the thinly-padded wall behind the basket. I wasn't about to drive the lane through traffic inside a prison. Let the math teacher break his neck. I moved in to ten feet and tried different angles. The court was so narrow I didn't think I'd get much off from the corners anyway.

The prisoner team jogged in through a door opposite us, escaping a locker room I didn't even want to imagine. I was sure each one of my teammates was absorbing two things: all of the prisoners were black; one of them was a life-size replica of the NBA's man-child, Darryl Dawkins. What else I noticed? After giving us the once-over in return, none of the convicts acted as if they expected us to make this game interesting.

I felt the same way. Players no taller than my 6'2" loped to the basket and jammed the ball through with ease. The big guy, despite his bulk, casually crushed a slam back over his head. "You'll get a poem out of this," Pierce said. "Won't you?" He'd asked me once why what I wrote were called poems if none of them rhymed. Standing near the foul line with a ball cradled absently against my chest, it was all I could do to grunt "maybe" so he wouldn't ask again.

Two side doors opened, and the crowd filed in, every one of them black as well. It was a sociology lesson. Every guard that accompanied them was as white as we were. My Jim Crow legs felt heavy and soggy, but Pierce, apparently, was blind. He wound right into his pregame speech as if the other end of the court was dotted with clean-shaven, cow-licked farm boys. "We managed to get a game with their A Team," Pierce said.

"I talked you guys up enough to get a real challenge."

Right about then I didn't want a challenge. I wanted the B or even the C Team out there for the jump ball—five white guys with bad hands and no wind, the kind of team that would drop back into a sagging zone and concede my eighteen foot jump shot with only a few waves of its tattooed arms. Pierce was an idiot to have claimed we were anything but over-educated. Certainly, I could see clearly that all of my swearing and beer-swilling in college had done nothing but camouflage my innate gutlessness.

For the opening tip, the convicts sent out a thin, twitchy guy who looked to be about 5'9". Our West Virginia football alum was about 6'5", but he didn't get much air under his sneakers. The stands buzzed approval for what looked to be the first of many humiliations, and they got their wish when the little guy cleanly tapped the ball to the Darryl Dawkins look-a-like. He whirled and found a teammate who drove uncontested to the basket, but because that guy, who looked to be my size, turned a 180 and tried to jam behind his head, the ball banged off the back rim and carried directly to my office mate. From where I stood, not having moved since the ball had left the referee's hands, I trotted down court as if all of this had been choreographed.

For six minutes, incredibly, we built a lead. 14-6, the scoreboard read, and the convicts took a time out. They were leading in righteous moves and attempted dunks, but no one had taken a routine shot. Worse, they were going for every head fake as if they were chemistry professors anticipating the first clean block of their lives during a lunch time scrimmage. And somehow I'd hit three out of four from medium range, rising to shoot while the guy guarding me was falling back to earth.

"Anybody winded?" Pierce said in the huddle. The math guy was bouncing. Somebody along the bench said, "We're kicking their asses" so loudly I worried the A team might have heard.

As it turned out, the team that returned for the convicts had enlarged itself. Now they had three enforcers inside and two serious-looking guys outside, one of which, when I made my one move—fake left, go right, and pull up—never flinched. He slapped at the ball, catching my wrist, but there was no call. I had to let my shot go without getting my feet squared, and barely caught iron. "Shit, white bread," the guy said, following me down court like a shadow, "you been read."

The prisoners set up a series of picks, delivering forearms, throwing hips, everything away from the ball. There was only one referee, and they freed cutters for layups until it was 16-16 and Pierce made an emphatic T with his hands. "You drowning now, white bread," my shadow said as we turned toward our benches. "You in over your head."

The math guy was up and ready. "Ok," Pierce declared, "you're in. We need somebody to fight through screens. We need some hustle. We need some get up and go."

Two minutes later we were down by seven, and I had the ball stripped and slam-dunked through what was, by now, the far distant basket. "You dead, white bread," my shadow said so softly I thought for a moment he was being kind. Only the math guy chased after, so he tried a long baseball pass that was intercepted, and he found himself facing a two-on-one, the second slam in eight seconds bouncing off his shoulder as the gym rocked with high-fives. "Yo, bread," I heard to my left a few seconds later, so I turned right and fed the math guy, who went on a kamikaze run at the hoop, getting the ball tipped from the side so it bounced against a knee and caromed loose in the lane.

The convicts' big guy surged out of the crowd with it, no surprise, but he was holding his eye as if he could feel pain. "Motherfucker!" he yelled, and swung an elbow that caught the jump ball artist flush, snapping his head back and laying him out on the floor. "Motherfucker!" the big guy roared again, and everybody backed off, opening a circle around what looked to be a dead man.

Pierce managed to keep his coach's reflexes. He motioned us to the bench. I sat down first and said, "I'm beat" at once. "Put somebody in."

"Somebody goes in for me," Pierce said. "I'm the one poked the big fella in the eye."

"They have one cold-cocked guy out there," my office mate offered. "They have themselves an incident."

The down time stretched. The Darryl Dawkins guy walked to the bench, covering one eye like a man taking a vision test on the move. Soon only the unconscious player was left on the court. When I picked up some movement in the bleachers behind me, I stood up like I'd found my second wind, but it was only two prison guards stationing themselves in the open row between us and the crowd that looked, suddenly, like a comically ineffective moat.

The downed player began to make pedaling motions with his legs as the referee approached Pierce. "You want to call it a day?" he said.

Instead of taking a vote, Pierce said, "No way."

"I can't protect you out there," the referee confessed. "I can't guarantee anything."

Pierce nodded. "We understand," he said, freely using the collective pronoun.

The recovering player was sitting up by now, shaking out the cobwebs. I imagined him listening to the buzz of a million trapped flies just before he stood and shuffled to the bench. "You be whooped now, white bread," I heard the first time I touched the ball. "Your woman good in bed?"

I wondered if Pierce, dribbling a few feet away, had heard. There was poetry he recognized here all right, but for me, by then, it was a narrative of difference, the metaphors of boundaries, including the one created by a phalanx of white prison guards. For the rest of the half I shot nothing but NBA-style three-pointers before I could get stripped again. We were down thirteen at the half, a testament to the convicts' inability to convert offensive rebounds.

Back in the locker room I watched a centipede as long as my thumb emerge from under a locker. There had to be more, I thought, though it was wise enough to retreat so only its head was visible. "We're in this thing," Pierce was ranting like Custer, but by now, except for the math instructor, there weren't any soldiers or schoolboys in the room with him.

"One of the guards protecting our backs said the big guy caved in somebody's head with a cue stick," my office mate said. "Manslaughter is what he's serving time for. He's up for parole in less than a year."

"Let's stall," I said. "Let's hold the ball until he's back in the world." In the silence that followed I noticed the centipede was gone.

"Let's listen to coach," the math professor said, and I stared at him, remembering that Pierce had once told me that he worked out every day, that he'd told Pierce his biggest fear, at thirty-two, was getting out of shape.

"Come on," he said again, "let's do it for coach," and Pierce slapped him on the back.

"Corn bread," I thought, but the rhyme didn't come to me.

With five minutes left we were down by twenty-three, and Pierce emptied the bench. I sat down with fifteen points and one accidental rebound. We lost by thirty-four. The guards opened the doors for the crowd, and they filed out in a way that surprised me with its deference. I shook hands with three of the other players, missing the guy who'd called me out with simple rhymes. He'd disappeared before I'd dragged myself off the bench where I'd listened to Pierce shout encouragement to the makeshift team he'd put on the floor.

I didn't chance my bare feet on the floor of the gang shower. I toweled off as best I could and turned everything in my locker inside out and shook it before I put it back on.

Outside it was snowing. Just flurries, but threatening worse, Sunday afternoon turned dismal, dark clouds amplifying the twilight of February's early sunset. I waited until my office mate slid into the car Pierce was driving, then opened the door of the other. I'd heard enough chatter for one day.

When my next thought was that I felt released, I was embarrassed for myself. The driver, a computer science instructor, worried aloud about whether the road might turn slick. As soon as he turned on the radio to search for a forecast, the trivial words of a set of sponsors welcomed me back into the world.

THE MUSSOLINI DIARIES

In 1957, a mother and daughter produced 30 volumes of what they claimed were Benito Mussolini's diaries. The older woman, it turned out, had perfected Mussolini's handwriting, duplicating it well enough to fool Mussolini's son and the requisite university expert, who exclaimed, after examining the diaries, "Thirty volumes of manuscript cannot be the work of a forger, but of a genius."

The fraud progressed well enough to gather attention and embarrass a number of people, something like the later, more publicized Hitler Diaries fiasco. Except the *Sunday Times of London*, eleven years after the forgery was exposed, bought, from those same women, $71,400 worth of pages to publish.

An extraordinary lapse of memory or research, although, in 1983, the daughter resurfaced to deny she and her mother had forged any of those thirty volumes, reasserting the authenticity of the diaries a generation after they were first exposed. Looking for yet another buyer, perhaps, or one more expert to nod approval, she insisted the original confession was coerced. Everybody knows such things happen, she said, that we're not responsible for what we say under pressure. Who knows what the police will do to us, what we'll be offered to confess?

Our third grade teacher, Miss Klein, told us it was time to master cursive, starting with ovals repeated across the page. "Around, around, around," she chanted, and we all managed. We earned our inkwells; we jammed the steel points into place and held pens ready to write. Dip, swirl, and don't rest the tip on the paper. We had to master the Peterson Method unless we wanted to be fools like the printers and inkwell spillers, the stained ones who were going to be failures, on relief, heading straight for the trailer court or the North Side soup kitchens we passed on our field trips.

We had blotters from the bank, last month stamped on each one as they were passed back the row. When March was distributed — a comic wind ineffective against a secure vault — we changed to cursive for every assignment we handed in. We wrote a letter to our parents, signing our names. We'd practiced and practiced on our tablets, perfecting those signatures, and I'd signed my name where it said BOOK OWNER on the inside covers of the multiple copies of a history book I found on the shelves in the back of the room, repeating it like a serial I expected to become a novel. I couldn't wait for that letter, which I imagined to be a preface to the history of my life, to reach my house. There was nothing I was unwilling to record, wondering if one alphabet, in cursive, was enough, if my name was legible in all thirty-five books, or disconnected somehow, from the evolution of ovals, webbed strangely like fingers which pronounce ourselves.

In the newspaper, a man sits with his wallet, its papers and cards fanned across a desk. "Stolen," he says, "at the physical I took for World War II." He's arranged the old pictures as if for a seance, calling up the ghosts from the black and white of seventy years ago, all of those decades lost in the attic of a thief, in a locked black box, perhaps, kept with a thousand other stolen wallets. The pay rate on his wage stub seems slavery; the creased-note woman has thinned and died; the boy in one picture is looking at the camera like the treed bear in the photograph below. Hunger, the article says, drew it here, too close to town, and the bear stares at the people-rings which spread from its tree as if the oak were quivering in water, as if that water, bewildered, rippled endlessly, unknowable as reasons for returning a wallet, believing in an address seventy years after theft, that someone would forward it, that someone would open it, amazed, and whisper, "Jesus, Son of Mary, this is mine."

In seventeenth century England, a religious allegory was published. Entitled *A Wordless Book*, it totaled eight blank pages: two black for evil, two red for redemption, two white for purity, two gold for eternal bliss.

In 1738, Herman Boerhaave died and left one copy of a self-published, sealed book, *The Onliest and Deepest Secrets of the Medical Art*. The book sold for $20,000 at auction and, when the new owner opened it, everything but the title page was blank.

More recently, Thomas Wirgman arranged his self-published books by page color. He spent $200,000 to produce his work, trying to get the sequence of colors exactly right. Purple, orange, blue, yellow, brown — a possibly sublime first chapter, a pattern to engage all readers. Yellow, green, red, green, yellow, blue. Altogether, he sold six copies, misunderstood, perhaps, like a genius.

Now, the salesman who wants me to buy a blank book, each of its leather-bound pages white, says they mitigate grief. "Turn the pages slowly," he says. "Linger a bit on each one. You'll see."

My daughter tells me she's met a student who was ecstatic about her first publication. She was in France; her mother had called from the United States to tell her the news. She had been sending out letters to editors for several years, reading magazines at random and submitting thousands of letters on whatever subject moved her to write. She was perfecting the epistolary mode, sending to weeklies, monthlies, and quarterlies. "I'm a writer," she said. "And now I have my first credit."

Once, Gandhi wrote a letter to Charles Atlas, asking, "I wonder if there is some way you can build me up?" He wanted to try Dynamic Tension, the science of pitting one muscle against another. And because Atlas, as he claims, felt sorry "for the poor chap, nothing but a bag of bones," he sent Gandhi his instructions for free.

When I was a senior in college, a man jostled his bar stool closer and told me, as soon as I turned, he could tell my fortune. I said "Sure thing" and started picking pages from the fresh issue of *Life* he'd laid on the bar. "This weekly is infallible as the Bible," he said. "Choose four pages with no ads, and the numbers will tell you your job, your wife's name, how many children you'll have, and the city where you'll live the longest."

And why not, I thought, because I wasn't reading anymore, watching my life-to-be on the television news, waiting for a pizza, a drink, and the draft. I wasn't a pacifist. I wasn't crippled or criminal or employed at anything vital. I paid for his beer and mine and fluttered the pages so I could choose, for once, tomorrow at random: Salesman and Sarah, none and Cleveland. I said "thanks" like I should have, and for "you're welcome" he insisted me back to *Life* to fill my skeptic hand with the number of the year I'd die. And what the hell, I flipped to "This one" and watched him drink and run his fingers down the Tet-Offensive text until he smiled and clapped me on the back, laughing at the lifeline he'd counted down for me, the two of us laughing, then, like fortunate friends safe in their jobs and homes and health, and I didn't believe anything that prophet was saying.

During the reign of Ming emperor Yung Lo (1402–1424), an 11,095 volume encyclopedia was compiled and written. Because of its length, it was too expensive to be published.

Hendrik Hertzberg produced a book called *One Million*. In varying numbers, each chapter consisted entirely of dots.

The 1886 *Appletons' Cyclopædia of American Biography* contained 84 phony biographies submitted by an unknown correspondent. For years, some of those entries stayed. It took until 1936 to weed out the final fraud.

My mother cleaned up crime with food — bacon and eggs, toast, grapefruit sections she carved out while I showered the dry heaves away like sin. "You eat your breakfast," she said, and I managed, one slow mouthful at a time, wiping the grease and soft yolk with bread until I could see my face in that spotless plate. How light it was in July, though not yet six a.m., the time when I drove back to Pittsburgh and the first shift at Heinz.

"You make a mess of yourself," my father said, "don't come crying to me." My mother said, "You come home in one piece."

That summer I stole the letter to my parents from the registrar who quantified one mess I'd made. I changed the F I'd received for Fine Arts to a B and retallied my quality points, my credits, and my grade point average. Those numbers were difficult to work with, and I added up fictitious sums in columns crowded close to the typed numbers I'd altered. As if I were figuring alternate grade points. As if I were anticipating one of my final grades being changed by a sympathetic or careless professor. Something to account for all those diversions, each of them a possible improvement, each a reason not to look closely at the lies I'd created because they were temporary and certain to be improved.

Unless my father somehow learned I'd failed that course and refused to pay my tuition, the theft meant I had a semester to clean up my grades. Now I had the opportunity to say "See?" and show the following two years of Dean's Lists, the advanced degrees I said I'd earn if I got away with those necessary lies.

I smiled when I read about the Septuagint, how there were 72 translators, six from each of the 12 tribes of Israel who worked in separate rooms, and when they finished, when they compared, all of their work was identical. But today, all of the newspapers in the library began with the same sentence; today, each of the 12 channels on my father's television showed the same celebrity's face because he was accused of murder.

The valentine of coincidence is bordered by old doilies: Some numerologists claim Shakespeare helped write the Bible. The evidence: The King James Version was published in 1610 when Shakespeare was 46 years old; Shake is the 46th word of Psalm 46; Spear is the 46th word from the end of Psalm 46.

Our house held a dozen Bibles — King James, the Revised, one with a thick concordance. They lay open to highlighted verses, stood closed beside photographs of owners long dead and delivered to promises or deceit. Every word in each was true and perfect and surged through the filaments of my body until I glowed with hope. I breathed the dust of generations gone to glory. I memorized, word for word, scriptures selected for the growing boy.

Vortigern and Rowena is the title of a play William Henry Ireland claimed was written by Shakespeare. Ireland forged love letters from Shakespeare to Anne Hathaway; he wrote the cursive script for a drawer full of personal papers, convincing James Boswell, among others, of their authenticity. And that play was performed at the Drury Lane Theater in 1796, jeered by the audience, who knew Shakespeare, apparently, better than handwriting analysts did, insuring it would never be performed again.

For years a man named William Key has claimed the word SEX is visible in Lincoln's beard on every five dollar bill. For America's confidence, Key explains. It's there as a subliminal surge reminding us to save or spend, with ease, our currency. He's published directions to its sighting, and I've followed his map to ink blots which, on every one of the fifty five-dollar bills I've tested, have spelled nothing.

"The history of passion will tumble this week," I read, Pennsylvania slicing off the dangerous scales of the crumbling cliff where rockslides threaten one of its highways.

The newspaper suggests a reunion, asking former defacers to gather for an hour, and I park off Route 28, north of Pittsburgh, to read the graffiti of desire.

There are dozens of cars, perhaps fifty of us looking up at the hand-over-hand history of lust, and I try to pick out Doreen and Clarice, Monica and Donna, reading nearby faces like name tags at a conference, deciding whether or not they're still paired with Chuck and Ron, Woody and Buck.

I think Gary sounds so formal I'm the fool who was never in love, that Gary + Sharon, still visible, is a forgery because only the Butch I once was would have risked himself seventy feet above this traffic, that nobody else at the base of this blackboard would have struggled into danger and printed anything but his nickname before he added the full spelling of the girl he'd stay with forever.

160

Alcibiades Simonides, during the 19th Century, forged a manuscript of Homer, sold it to the king of Greece, who first consulted scholars at the University of Athens, each of them saying "Yes" to authenticity.

In Sharpsburg, a Dairy Queen has become The Lighthouse Bible Baptist Church. The signboard's letters spell times and themes and ALL WELCOME under the multiple ramps of the bypass. The church bulletin replaces the menu as if you could bend to the sliding glass window to order salvation.

Leaving it behind, I search for the Greenwood Cemetery. It's been twenty-five years, and I try two wrong roads before I'm lucky with a third. I park by the tallest monument, which is dedicated to local Civil War veterans, those from Sharpsburg, Etna, and vicinity under George Custer. At its base are five other medals for later wars, none of them served under a name I recognize, and I walk left of the huge patch of flags before I turn right to a swath of Langs and Hemkes in this cemetery above Sharpsburg. It's the side of the family all dead or moved away but my sister, one step on my private route through reunion weekend.

Four of these gravesites are flowering, four are not. The geraniums bloom red for my grandmother, two great uncles and one aunt; the other four relatives lie bare. My sister, when I tell her the story later, says, "That's the way I always do it." As if she were singing a chorus after verses I'm supposed to know for the ballad of the favored, how they were thought of entering the earth.

A student tells me he's transcribed thousands of words from H. P. Lovecraft because the language he used made him the world's greatest writer. "Necrosis," he reads from the notebook he's holding. "Mephitic. Nobody else could ever think of those."

Greatness by way of medical dictionaries, I say, and repeat "emesis" and "lavage," two ways to rid characters of the possession of poisons.

He writes both words down as if a story were beginning.

Ern Malley, in 1944, was published in *Angry Penguins*, a magazine which proclaimed him as one of two giants of Australian poetry. He had just died at 25, the large selection of his poems submitted by his grieving sister. Each one of those poems had been copied, bits and pieces of various books pasted together by two bored soldiers.

When Nancy Luce wrote poems, she inscribed them on the eggs she gathered, adding the name, when she finished, of the chicken who'd laid that tablet. Like a dedication, since all of her poems were about those chickens she raised and loved. A sort of Psalms in praise of chickens. Verses have been embossed, too, on pins, carved into the walls of caverns and tombs. Poems have been traced in water, fire, and air, left untranscribed as the spark for the Big Bang. My father refuses his meals without the brief poem of prayer. He grips my visitor's hand and recites the rhymed passages of praise and thanks as if I'd gobble that food while he spoke, as if I'd join his recital over the bacon and eggs which welcome morning.

A criminal named George Cudmore, in 1830, was executed. His skin was used to bind a book, Milton's *The Poetical Works*, someone's notion of the odd possession.

Clifford Irving, in 1971, deceived five handwriting experts hired by his book publisher. All of them agreed it was the genuine Howard Hughes who wrote the supporting documents to verify the authenticity of the interviews for the forthcoming biography. For Irving to forge such an amount of material "would be beyond human ability," said one expert.

The photographic memory champion lives in Burma, reciting, so far, seventeen thousand pages of Buddhist books. He's memorized all of those volumes; someone else is compelled to read along for verification.

On the last afternoon of her life my mother wrote and mailed her weekly news to me. After the funeral, after travel, I received her note from the neighbor who'd held my mail. That letter lay warm in my hands; it yellowed and curled from the air I was drawing toward me and the language on the page. The signature in flames, I saw the return address affixed in the envelope's corner as it's supposed to be, insurance against loss.

ACKNOWLEDGMENTS

Essays in this collection previously appeared in:

Kenyon Review: "The Physics of Desire"
Arts & Letters: "Catching"
The Georgia Review: "Opening the Bone"
Pleiades: "The Simple Simile for Medicine"
The Southern Review: "Marking the Body"
PA English and *The Cresset:* "The Darkness Call"
Southern Humanities Review: "Subsidence, Mine Fire, the Tomb of Eve"
Brevity: "During the Farm Show Parade"
North Dakota Quarterly: "The History of Lie Detection"
Shenandoah: "Things that Fall from the Sky"
Black Warrior Review: "The Mussolini Diaries"
SmokeLong: "Yams"
Iron Horse Literary Review: "Dragging the Forest"
december: "Proximity"
Shenandoah: "A Punishment Seminar"
Southern Humanities Review: "Self-Defense"
Fast Break to Line Break: Poets on the Art of Basketball: "The Simple Rhymes of Defense"
Lake Effect: "Thoreau's Cane"
Cimarron Review: "Inexplicable"

"Dragging the Forest" was reprinted in *The Best of Iron Horse*

The following essays were cited as *Best American Essays* "Notable Essays": "Proximity" (2016), "The Physics of Desire" (2015), "The History of Lie Detection" (2011), "Subsidence, Mine Fire. The Tomb of Eve" (1999), "A Punishment Seminar" (1997)

ABOUT THE AUTHOR

Gary Fincke has published thirty-one books of poetry, short fiction, and nonfiction, most recently *The Out-of-Sorts: New and Selected Stories* (2017) and *Bringing Back the Bones: New and Selected Poetry* (2016). Winner of the Flannery O'Connor Award for Short Fiction and the Ohio State University/The Journal Poetry Prize, he has published work in such periodicals as *The Paris Review, The Missouri Review, Newsday, The Georgia Review, The Kenyon Review, Poetry, Black Warrior Review,* and *Crazyhorse.* He has been twice awarded Pushcart Prizes for his work, recognized by *Best American Stories* and the O. Henry Prize series, and cited fifteen times in the past eighteen years for a "Notable Essay" in *Best American Essays.* He has just retired as the Charles Degenstein Professor of English and Creative Writing at Susquehanna University.

THE ROBERT C. JONES PRIZE FOR SHORT PROSE

Robert C. Jones was a professor of English at University of Central Missouri and an editor at Mid-American Press who supported and encouraged countless young writers throughout a lifetime of editing and teaching. His legacy continues to inspire all of us who live, write, and support the arts in mid-America.

The editors at Pleiades Press select 10-15 finalists from among those manuscripts submitted each year. A judge of national renown selects one winner for publication.

ALSO AVAILABLE FROM PLEIADES PRESS

Among Other Things: Essays by Robert Long Foreman

Bridled by Amy Meng

A Lesser Love by E. J. Koh

In Between: Poetry Comics by Mita Mahato

Novena by Jacques J. Rancourt

Book of No Ledge: Visual Poems by Nance Van Winckel

Landscape with Headless Mama by Jennifer Givhan

Random Exorcisms by Adrian C. Louis

Poetry Comics from the Book of Hours by Bianca Stone

The Belle Mar by Katie Bickham

Sylph by Abigail Cloud

The Glacier's Wake by Katy Didden

Paradise, Indiana by Bruce Snider

What's this, Bombardier? by Ryan Flaherty

Self-Portrait with Expletives by Kevin Clark

Pacific Shooter by Susan Parr

It was a terrible cloud at twilight by Alessandra Lynch

Compulsions of Silkworms & Bees by Julianna Baggott

Snow House by Brian Swann

Motherhouse by Kathleen Jesme

Lure by Nils Michals

PLEIADES
P R E S S